'I must be insane,' Jonas breathed raggedly.

'You're a member of my staff and a junior one at that. I should be training you, guiding you, not seducing you! Your father would have a fit if he knew...'

'For goodness' sake, Jonas,' Gemma flung back angrily. 'I coped with the pain and trauma of a middle third fracture to my face and then went on to medical school where I also coped, and now I'm holding down a job, so why all the fuss?'

'It's a matter of ethics,' he said flatly. 'Professional *and* sexual.'

Abigail Gordon is fascinated by words, and what better way to use them than in the crafting of romance between the sexes—a state of the heart that has affected almost everyone at some time of their lives? Twice widowed, she now lives alone in a Cheshire village. Her two eldest sons between themselves have presented her with three delightful grandchildren, and her youngest son lives nearby.

Recent titles by the same author:

DR BRIGHT'S EXPECTATIONS
POLICE SURGEON

SAVING FACES

BY
ABIGAIL GORDON

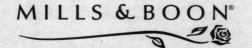

For my granddaughter Gemma Alicia Brook

*First published in Great Britain 2000
Harlequin Mills & Boon Limited,
Eton House, 18-24 Paradise Road, Richmond, Surrey TW9 1SR*

© Abigail Gordon 2000

ISBN 0 263 82242 7

*Set in Times Roman 10½ on 11½ pt.
03-0006-54029*

*Printed and bound in Spain
by Litografia Rosés, S.A., Barcelona*

CHAPTER ONE

THERE was still an hour to go before she needed to leave the house but Gemma was ready. In a grey tailored suit with a collarless white blouse, sheer black tights and expensive leather shoes of the same colour, she looked more like a young business executive than a junior doctor at the beginning of another gruelling week on the wards.

'Gee whiz! Gemma, girl! You *do* look smart,' her father said as he came downstairs to find her pacing up and down the lounge. 'But why are you up so early? Couldn't you sleep?'

'No, I couldn't, Pops,' she admitted. 'It's today that Jonas Parry is taking over the plastic surgery unit and I want to make a good impression.'

Harry Bartlett eyed his dark-haired daughter quizzically. 'And the thought of that kept you awake?'

'Mmm. Crazy, aren't I?'

The retired GP smiled. 'Not really. I know how you feel about the fellow. But you're not expecting him to remember you, surely? It's almost ten years ago. You were a teenager with an injured face...one of dozens he will have treated during his climb to the top.'

'Maybe he *won't* remember me,' she conceded, 'but that isn't the most important thing. What Jonas Parry did for me changed the direction of my life, as well as saving my looks.

'Whereas before I'd been undecided about going into medicine, after the accident my mind was made up. Not only was I sure it was what I wanted to do, but I knew that I wanted to specialise in plastic surgery and, after doing the rounds with various consultants, I've finally managed to get myself transferred to that particular unit.'

She wasn't going to tell her father that it wasn't just gratitude for the way the man had repaired her damaged face that had made him linger in her memory.

His hair had been dark bronze and cropped short around the most memorable face she'd ever seen. He'd laughed a lot. She remembered him teasing the nurses and joking with the patients, so that the horrendous problems some of them had had to cope with hadn't seemed quite so frightening after all.

Yet he'd had his serious side, too. As her youthful heartbeats had quickened because of him, Gemma had sobbed into her pillow each night in the darkened ward because he was seeing her at her ugliest. But almost as if he'd guessed what had been going through her mind, Jonas Parry had appeared at the side of her bed one night and with his dark hazel eyes full of calm confidence had looked down into hers and had told her that he was going to make her beautiful again...and he had.

He had repaired the damage to her face which had occurred when a school friend who had just passed her driving test had invited her to go for a ride—with disastrous results.

They'd crashed into an oncoming car and where the young driver had escaped unhurt, Gemma had suffered facial fractures and deep lacerations.

At the time she and her parents had been living in the Midlands and it was when she'd been transferred to the plastic surgery unit at one of the big hospitals there that she'd found herself being treated by Jonas Parry.

He wasn't the top man, just a member of a dedicated and very skilful team, but she worshipped him.

However, if Gemma had thought in her youthful ignorance that the restoration of her looks would attract the charismatic plastic surgeon, she'd been wrong.

On the very day that she was able to look in the mirror without cringing one of the nurses told her that Dr Parry was shortly to marry Paula Erskine whose father had a high position in the area health authority.

The news brought her feelings into perspective. She should have known that someone like Jonas Parry wouldn't look at a seventeen-year-old schoolgirl like herself. and when her parents came to take her home she couldn't get away quickly enough.

And now, her youthful crush relegated to the far distant past, she was going to meet him again...the man who had saved her face, but this time in a very different capacity. She would be on his side of the fence—on a much lower scale, admittedly, but in the business of saving the faces, the bodies...and in some circumstances the sanity of the sick and injured admitted to the big London hospital where she was at present employed as a junior doctor.

As her father bustled into the kitchen to start his methodical breakfast routine, Gemma ran her fingers over the smooth contours of her face with tapering fingers—high cheek-bones beneath dark almond eyes, a mouth that could tighten with determination just as quickly as curve into laughter and a small straight nose.

They were all features that went to make it beautiful, but in that moment she wasn't seeing them in her mind's eye. It was someone else's face, as clear in her mind now as it had been all that time ago, that was blocking her vision.

If her father thought she was dressed up to the nines for a Monday morning on the wards he was right, but no one knew better than he that the smart suit would be covered by a white coat within minutes of presenting herself.

But there was the time it would take her to park and make her way to the part of the hospital where she would be working and, junior doctor or not, if she were to meet Jonas Parry *en route* she was determined to look her best.

The frightened, suffering schoolgirl had been transformed into a confident young doctor, ready and willing to follow in his footsteps. That being the case, why were there butterflies in her stomach, instead of her usual hearty breakfast?

'You could go places in plastic surgery if you give your every waking thought to it,' Andrew Soames, the head of the unit had said to her some weeks previously when she'd been allowed into Theatre to observe a breast reconstruction after a mastectomy. 'I shall watch your progress with interest.'

But the busy, middle-aged consultant hadn't been able to do that. A desperate domestic situation facing his in-laws had made a move to another part of the country imperative for him and his family, and his replacement was due to take over today. Whether Jonas Parry would be as impressed with her abilities as Andrew had been was something that remained to be seen.

Lunchtime had arrived and there had been neither sight nor sound of the new man, and as Gemma made her way to the staff restaurant for a quick lunch one of the registrars she worked with caught her up.

Peter French was a sardonic, very average doctor, who had made some snide remarks about her being teacher's pet when Andrew Soames had been in charge, and now he was directing his barbs at their absent new chief.

'Parry is here, you know,' he said from behind as they queued up at the self-service counter, 'but obviously not yet ready to start mixing with the likes of us. They're all the same, these high flyers, only interested in hobnobbing with the top brass.'

'He's not like that!' she said quickly, and immediately wished she'd kept quiet.

'And how would *you* know what he's like? Already acquainted, are you?' he sneered.

'No, it's just what I've heard,' Gemma told him lamely.

She wasn't going to tell him that her defence of Jonas Parry came from what she'd seen for herself, rather than been told second hand.

And as for the rest of it, they *weren't* acquaintances. When eventually the new consultant put in an appearance he wouldn't know her from Adam, but she would know him. That was as sure as night following day.

At three o'clock that afternoon Gemma was moving swiftly along the main corridor of the hospital with a sheaf of notes in her hand when a voice from behind said abruptly, 'You've dropped something.'

She swivelled round in surprise and saw that she had indeed discarded an object along the way. As she bent to retrieve it she was relieved to see that it wasn't a loose sheet from the notes she was carrying.

Meticulous in everything she did, mislaying or losing paperwork wasn't something she'd ever been guilty of, but a plastic tyrannosaurus rex wasn't what was usually to be found in the pocket of her hospital coat and it had fallen out with a rubbery thud onto the tiled floor of the corridor.

As she straightened up Gemma became still. Had the moment she'd been waiting for all day arrived? Incredibly, she wasn't sure.

The eyes looking her over weren't the warm hazel orbs she remembered. They were like cold brown slate, and the laughing mouth she had yearned to kiss all that time ago was straight and uncompromising.

His hair was the same thick, burnished bronze as before,

but it had a slicked-down look about it and, incredibly, there was silver in it.

It *was* Jonas Parry, of course it was, but in the same moment that she acknowledged the fact Gemma thought, somebody, or something, had put out his fire.

But it was ten years since she'd last seen him. She was a fool to think he wouldn't have changed in that time because she had…for the better, she liked to think, whereas in his case it was like looking at a shell and an empty one at that.

As she stood uncomfortably with the plastic dinosaur in her hand it was a far cry from how she'd expected their moment of meeting to be. She had visualised him striding into the ward to find her the epitome of slender white-coated efficiency as she went about her duties, not a meeting in the corridor which was like having a bucket of cold water poured over her.

'One of my young patients must have put it in my pocket,' she said with a weak smile.

'So it would seem, Gemma Bartlett,' he replied with cold crispness as he took in the name on her badge.

She was eyeing him expectantly. Would the name ring a bell? Obviously not, as he was saying without any show of interest, 'I'm Jonas Parry. As of today I'm in charge of plastic surgery.'

'Yes, I know.'

The cold brown eyes were questioning. 'You know what? That I'm Jonas Parry? Or that Jonas Parry is taking over the plastic surgery unit? Or both?'

'I know that someone called Jonas Parry is to be the new head of the unit where I'm working,' she hedged, having decided that if he didn't recognize her there was no point in claiming a previous acquaintance. Her father had been right. He must have treated scores of teenagers with facial injuries.

'So you're going to be one of my lot, are you?' he commented. 'How long have you been on the unit?'

'Not long enough,' she told him candidly. 'It's what I've always wanted to do, but I've only recently got the chance.'

He sighed and glanced at his watch. I'm obviously boring him, she thought. If he's been with the hierarchy all morning, small talk with a junior doctor won't seem very exciting.

'Shall I direct you to the wards?' she offered, and he almost smiled.

'I *can* read. The place is well signposted. When you've given the T. rex back to its owner maybe you will join me there as I want to introduce myself to the staff and at the same time hold a briefing, where I shall explain my plans and policies for the unit.'

'Yes, of course,' she agreed meekly, and with deep disappointment blotting out any other feelings that the unexpected meeting might have conjured up she went on her way.

After taking a short cut, she was back on the ward before he arrived, and when she informed the nurses that his appearance was imminent there was much scuttling around and straightening of beds and uniforms.

Peter French, the registrar, was eyeing them disdainfully. 'So you've already met the new guy?' he said. 'What's he like?'

She was going through the notes at the bottom of the nearest patient's bed and didn't look up as she replied, 'On par with an iceberg.'

If she was expecting a comment from the sarcastic registrar it wasn't forthcoming. As she lifted her head in the silence that followed, Gemma saw that he'd moved away and his place had been taken by the iceberg in question.

The ward sister was hovering at his side, and from the

flush on her face and the increased coldness in his brown gaze it was clear that they had both heard her comment.

Gemma turned away. So what? It was true. The laughing saviour of her looks and self-esteem had gone and in his place was…what? A tough nut? A career climber?

If it was the latter, positions in plastic surgery didn't come any more coveted than being in charge of the unit in this big London hospital. Maybe that was how getting to the top had affected him. Power and prestige had turned him into a colder version of the man she'd known before.

'So? Went the day well?' her father asked that evening the moment she walked into the house.

Gemma wrinkled the pert nose which had been a gift from God in the shape of Jonas Parry. 'No. It didn't go well at all,' she told him. 'He's changed, Dad. All stand-offish and horrible…and he heard me say something to that effect.'

Her father hid a smile. 'Oh, dear! So it wasn't a joyful reunion of the slavish worshipper and the face-saver? What has made him change, do you think?'

She shrugged tense shoulders. 'I don't know, but no doubt all will be revealed as time passes. He spoke to us briefly and it's clear that he knows what he's about, but I felt like telling him that excellence is only achieved by walking side by side with humanity.'

'But you didn't?'

She smiled for the first time since entering the house. 'Er…no. I'd already put my foot in it once. I didn't want to antagonise him any more, but…'

'Given the opportunity you will say your piece?' he finished off for her.

'You could say that,' she agreed laughingly, and with a lightening of her heart went to change before serving the meal her father had painstakingly prepared.

'What about *your* day?' she asked as they ate in the small dining room overlooking the garden that had been her mother's pride and joy until a sudden heart attack the previous year had snatched her from them.

'Oh, not too bad,' he said uncomplainingly.

Gemma knew that he was finding it hard going without her mother, and that an afternoon spent on the bowling green, poring over the crossword in the daily paper or changing his library books were just exercises in getting the day over.

The only thing that really gave him pleasure was calling in at the surgery where he had practised for the last nine years before his retirement and chatting to the staff there—in particular to the man who had been his junior partner, Roger Croft. He would be coming round tonight after surgery to play chess with her father, and then Harry would toddle off to bed, tactfully leaving Roger and Gemma alone beside the fire in the cold autumn night.

She wished he wouldn't. Roger wasn't the one for her. He was kind and reliable, a good doctor and a staunch friend to her father, but not someone who made her heart beat faster or her blood run warm, and sooner rather than later she was going to have to make that clear to them both, Roger *and* her dad.

Was it success that had soured Jonas Parry? Gemma pondered as she locked up, after bidding Roger a chaste goodnight. Because successful he was. His name was becoming synonymous with plastic surgery.

Yet, to be fair, she had to admit that there had been nothing 'sour' about him as he'd introduced himself to the staff that afternoon and followed the introductions with a brisk, brief chat about what he hoped to achieve with their help, and how essential it was that they work as a team, from the lowest of them to himself.

There had been none of the 'great I am' about him and

apart from Peter French, who had never been known to
show enthusiasm about anything, the new top man had been
well received.

Maybe a better description of him than 'sour' was
'damped down' because that was how he'd struck her—
like someone whose fire had been extinguished. And she
couldn't see any chance of a mere junior doctor rekindling
his flame.

But in any case the man was married, she reminded herself—to some woman whose father had been high up in
health care in the town where they'd lived when Gemma
had been injured in the car crash.

If Jonas Parry had been late in making an appearance on
his first day, he made up for it on his second. When Gemma
presented herself on the ward at eight-thirty she was informed that he was about to start his clinic and wanted a
junior doctor to assist him.

There were usually a couple of them on the ward, but
James Brice, a middle-aged latecomer to medicine, was on
sick leave, which left only herself, and it was with some
trepidation that she made her way to Outpatients.

If she'd been hoping that his bounce would have returned
she was to be disappointed. His manner was the same as
the previous day, cold, abrupt and contained, and if she'd
been on the defensive then, today she was doubly so.

When the first patient came in Gemma had stationed herself in a standing position behind him where she could listen and observe, but Jonas Parry said with a frown, 'You're
not going to be able to make any satisfactory diagnosis
from that distance. Come and sit beside me. I don't bite.'

No, you don't, she thought as she obeyed the order, but
you've certainly got a bark, and my powers of concentration won't be improved by being in such close proximity
to you.

The middle-aged woman, looking at them anxiously, had a grossly swollen leg, the skin of which was extremely thick and wart-ridden, and as they both eyed it keenly she said, 'The doctor I saw before said it was something to do with my lymph glands.'

'Yes, it is,' he agreed. 'It's a condition called lymphoedema where the lymph produced in your leg isn't draining away as it should through the lymphatic channels.'

It's also known as elephantiasis, Gemma thought, but he isn't going to elaborate on that as the issues associated with the name are frightening to say the least.

'I've had my leg in a special stocking and had it raised during the night, but it didn't help,' the patient was saying, 'and then they gave me a special sock to wear and a mechanical pump that I had to use for two hours each night as a form of compression, but my leg hasn't gone down any.'

Jonas nodded in agreement and, turning to Gemma, said, 'What would you suggest, Dr Bartlett?'

She hesitated. She'd read about it, but had never actually seen the condition until this moment.

'Diuretics, maybe?' she suggested.

He shook his head. 'No. Definitely not. If the previous treatment hasn't worked there has to be an obstruction somewhere.'

Facing the patient again, he said, 'I'm going to have you admitted to the plastic surgery unit. If tests show that I'm right, I'll operate to remove all the excess tissue that has formed due to the malfunction of the lymphatic vessels, and when that has been done I'll insert a skin flap deep into the leg muscle to repair the damage done by the cutting away of the surplus tissue.'

The colour had drained from the woman's face as she'd listened to what he had to say, and for a moment Gemma saw him as the man he'd been before—reassuring, positive and kind—as he took a workworn hand in his and said gently, 'Trust me. I'm going to make it right.'

Gemma watched the patient's face clear. The woman believed him...and so did she.

'Ever seen it before?' he asked when she'd gone.

Gemma shook her head. 'No, not in reality. I saw the film *Elephant Man* and that was gruesome.'

'Hmm. It was,' he agreed briefly, and then switched back to the matter they were discussing. 'The lady will need a week's preparation before I can operate. That's how long the physio and nurses will need to work on that skin to make it more supple.'

'What will they use?'

'Oil,' he said with continuing brevity, and told the nurse who was assisting them to bring in the next patient.

This time the problem was self-inflicted, but the man with a large unsightly tattoo on his arm was only concerned with a solution to his stupidity.

'What's the chances of getting it removed, Doc?' he wanted to know. 'My first wife didn't mind it, but I'm gettin' married again and she says the weddin' is off if I don't get rid of it.'

After Jonas had examined the density of the tattoo, he turned to Gemma and asked, 'What would *you* say is required in a case like this?'

With the memory of her recently discarded suggestion of diurectics for the elephantiasis, Gemma was more cautious this time.

'If the dye is as deep in the dermis as I think it might be, the whole area would need to be removed and a skin graft applied.'

The russet-haired consultant nodded his agreement this time, and with a warning glance at the possible recipient he took up where she'd left off by saying, 'Which would leave a permanent patch of different-textured skin on the arm.'

'Yeah, well, I'll have to put up with that, won't I?' the man said. 'When can you do it?'

Gemma hoped that Jonas would tell him that it would be if and when he had the time, for there were many people requiring his skills who hadn't asked for what *they'd* got.

He didn't let her down. Where the old Jonas might have administered a more pleasant reprimand, the new toughie told him straight.

'One of us on the plastic surgery unit will operate on you as we undertake cosmetic surgery, as well as treating the aftermath of accidents and malignancies, but be aware that as yours is not an urgent case you will have to wait your turn. It could be some months.'

'Months! What about my wedding?' the man complained.

'I'm sure that the lady will be willing to go ahead with it once she hears that you're on our waiting list,' Jonas said levelly, and with a nod to the hovering nurse to indicate that the consultation was over he sat back to await the arrival of the next patient.

Whatever Jonas had become, by the end of the morning Gemma knew that she enjoyed working with him. If he was brusque with adults, he wasn't so with children, and it was in his dealings with the little ones attending his clinic that she saw a glimpse of the man who had captured her girlish heart all that time ago.

Maybe she was imagining that he was different, she thought as the last outpatient departed. Perhaps he hadn't been as wonderful as she remembered. Yet if that were so, why had she cherished the memory of him for so long?

The obvious answer was because he'd put her face back together again but, grateful as she'd been, it hadn't been just that. Every time he'd appeared on the ward it had been like the sun coming from behind clouds. She'd sensed the joy of living in him and had tuned in to his humorous yet deep compassion.

She'd thought then that he would make a delightful husband and father, and maybe he was. If she were to tell him that they'd met before, shortly before his marriage, he might tell her what was going on in his life now. Ridiculous though it was, she had to know.

Incredibly, in a matter of seconds the opportunity presented itself for her to do that very thing. As she took off her hospital coat to go for lunch, the hanger at the back of it caught on the fine gold chain around her neck, and as she struggled to loosen it Jonas stepped forward to assist her.

As it came free he said slowly, 'You've had plastic surgery, Gemma Bartlett, haven't you?'

'Er...yes...' she mumbled. 'I was in a car crash when I was seventeen.'

'Who performed it?'

It would have been the easiest thing in the world to have said, You did, but the words stuck in her throat.

It hurt that he didn't remember her, though common sense told her he had no reason to. She'd been a skinny schoolgirl, and he'd been engaged to Paula Erskine, who'd turned out to be a cool, blonde, executive type when Gemma had checked her out.

What was she now? she wondered. One of the elegant working mum types, or a stay-at-home housewife in a large house who went to coffee mornings, did voluntary work and visited the beautician once a week?

'So?' he was asking, his brown eyes not as cold as yesterday. 'Are you going to tell me?'

It was then that she knew she didn't want him to know. Not yet, anyway.

'Er...I don't recall his name,' she fibbed.

'From one of the London hospitals, no doubt?'

'Yes, that's correct.'

That was two whoppers she'd just told and, having no wish for the score to go up to three, she opened the door, ready to depart.

But not yet!

'Hang on a moment,' Jonas said. 'If you're off to the restaurant I'm going there myself.'

'Tell me about yourself,' he said as they proceeded swiftly towards the smell of cooking.

'There's not much to tell,' Gemma said quietly. 'I live in Wimbledon with my father who's a retired GP. We lost my mother last year.'

'I see. I'm sorry.'

'I miss her more than words can say,' she told him with a catch in her voice.

'I'm sure you do,' he said sombrely and added as if he felt they might be on uneven ground, 'What made you take up medicine?'

'I'd always had the urge to go into health care but as I got to the age when a decision had to be made I was dithering a bit...that was until I was hospitalised myself. That experience helped me to make up my mind.'

'And having had plastic surgery, you were drawn towards that in particular?'

'Yes, you could say that.'

'No second thoughts?'

As she shook her head the dark swathe of her hair moved gently with it. 'No, never. Which, of course, doesn't mean that it won't have second thoughts about me. What about you, sir? Where do you live?' she asked quickly, to change the subject.

If he'd been thawing out, the ice was back.

'I have a flat in Pimlico.'

'And a house somewhere else?'

She was being incredibly nosy but couldn't help herself. A flat in a good area wasn't unusual for a top surgeon like him, but for some reason she was surprised.

'No, just the flat,' he said casually as they went through the swing doors of the restaurant together, and that was that.

The information she was hankering after came from another source...from the mouth of the unlikeable Peter French, and it came with his own particular brand of malicious relish.

'Guess what?' he said gloatingly as they did the rounds of the two plastic surgery wards together in the middle of the afternoon.

Gemma was checking that a young chef who had sustained full-thickness burns to the back of his hand was doing the necessary exercises to prevent stiffening of the injured area. She had watched Peter cover the burned part of the hand with silver sulphadiazine to prevent infection. Then they'd placed it in a sterile plastic bag in an elevated position, and now she was impressing upon the lad that he must keep up the movements as he had been instructed.

'What?' she asked absently, having satisfied herself that the patient understood the importance of what she'd been saying.

'I've discovered that our senior colleague lives with Michaela Martin, the actress, so *she* won't have to shop around when she needs a face-lift, will she?'

About to move on to the next bed, Gemma had stopped in her tracks and now she was swivelling slowly to face him, thinking dismally as she did so that she'd wanted to know what was going on in Jonas Parry's life and she was finding out with a vengeance.

'So, what about his wife?' she asked weakly.

'Wife? I don't know,' the registrar replied, his eyes glinting. 'Is he supposed to have one?'

Oh, dear! The last thing she wanted was for Peter to latch onto the fact that she'd met Jonas before.

She gave a careless shrug and hoped that it was convincing. 'I was taking it for granted that he was a married man, that's all. They usually are at his age. Take yourself, for instance.'

If she'd wanted to put him off the scent, the mention of his own affairs had done the trick.

He gave a derisive snort and Gemma knew that she was about to be regaled with a list of his woes and whingeings about the married state. However, it was a small price to pay if she'd sidetracked his interest in the man she'd imagined to be wrapped in family life.

So, Jonas was living with a beautiful actress. She'd seen Michaela Martin on television in a sizzling play only weeks before, and from what she'd observed it would be a long time before that one needed a face lift!

What had happened to the cool blonde he'd been about to marry all that time ago? she wondered. Separated? Divorced? Dead? She would dearly like to know.

Her parents had moved to the London area shortly after her recovery from the car crash. Subsequently she'd heard no more of the delightful doctor, and as she'd gone on to medical school her youthful crush on him had become just a magical memory.

As her adolescence had been left behind and she'd become a keen medical student, what would she have done if she'd known he was free? Pursued him? Hardly. He would still have seen her as a lesser mortal...just as he did now.

CHAPTER TWO

ON A chilly Tuesday evening three weeks later Gemma was in the local pub with her father, Roger, and Gary and Alison, the young couple who lived next door to them.

The five of them usually gathered there on Tuesday nights for a chat and a drink, although in her case it was as and when her job allowed.

She'd done a seventy-hour stint the previous week and was anticipating a repeat performance. Consequently, she was tired. It wasn't an unusual state of affairs for a junior doctor, but when given the chance she could always sleep herself back into a re-energised state, returning to the wards refreshed and raring to go.

But as well as being tired, she was feeling restless and depressed. She knew why, of course. As she looked around her at the cheerful crowd, Gemma thought that her social life was so boring it was almost non-existent.

And whose fault was that? The job didn't help, and when she did have some time to herself she was usually too tired to socialise, and if she wasn't, where was there to go?

This weekly gathering in the pub and the occasional night at the cinema with a girl friend was the limit of her recreational activities. Life was passing her by, she thought as she gazed at the sparkling white wine in her glass.

Yet she'd been contented enough until recently. It was only since Jonas had resurfaced in her life that she'd been feeling like this.

As if the twisted fates were out to emphasise further the difference in their lifestyles, the television set in the corner caught her eye.

It was the first night of an Andrew Lloyd Webber show at a large London theatre, and taxis were spilling out celebrities onto the pavements in front of the foyer.

A commentator, resplendent in evening dress, was identifying them for the benefit of the viewing public, and as Gemma watched the screen the cameras switched to a petite, golden-haired beauty in a designer gown, with her hand resting in the crook of the arm of the man beside her.

She looked stunning, but the eyes of the girl in the pub were on her companion, and a surge of shocked surprise mixed with envy swept over her as the man with the microphone said, 'Arriving at this moment is actress Michaela Martin, escorted by Jonas Parry, the plastic surgeon...the answer to the prayers of the wrinklies.'

Jonas was smiling. He looked happy and relaxed for once but, then, who wouldn't at such a gathering...and with such a companion? They made a striking pair. His tall figure and good looks were the perfect foil for his partner's blonde beauty.

It seemed as if Jonas hadn't heard the tasteless remark just made about him as there had been no change in his expression, but Gemma had and anger sparked inside her.

How dare the man describe the work Jonas did in such a manner? Only that day she'd been privileged to watch him treat a badly burned child, and as the plastic surgery team had fought to give meaning to a young life the importance of what they were doing had made her feel humble.

'I asked if you'd like another drink?' Roger's voice said in her ear.

'Oh, sorry,' she apologised. 'I saw someone I know on the television.'

'Who?'

'My boss.'

'Jonas Parry?'

'Er…yes. He was at the première of the new Lloyd Webber show.'

'Lucky guy,' he said casually. 'Who was he with?'

'Michaela Martin.'

'*Very* lucky guy!'

'Yes, indeed,' she agreed flatly.

When they got back to the house her father asked, 'What's wrong, Gemma? You've hardly spoken a word all night.'

She managed to dredge up a smile. 'I'm tired, Dad, that's all.'

He was eyeing her thoughtfully. 'You're sure it's nothing to do with Parry? I know how much you were looking forward to seeing him again.'

'You mean, am I still yearning after him?'

'Something like that.'

'Yes, I am, but I'm wasting my time. He's involved with a well-known actress.'

Harry sighed. 'Forget him, Gemma,' he advised gently. 'For one thing you reckon that he's not the same pleasant fellow that he was, and for another…there's Roger who dotes on you…hangs on your every word…not that you've had many to say tonight…but he really does care for you.'

The last thing she was in the mood for was the moment of truth that she'd kept promising herself, but it looked as if the time had come to put her father right about her feelings for Roger Croft.

'Maybe,' she conceded sombrely, 'but I don't care for him, not in that way, and, Dad, the sooner you and he accept that…the better.'

He sighed again. 'That was what I've been afraid you might say and it's all because of this ridiculous obsession you have with Jonas Parry. What's the point of falling in love with a man who doesn't even know you exist.'

'I'm not in love with him,' she cried angrily. 'It's just

that I admire and respect him above all other men, even if he isn't as upbeat as he was. Yet I do sense that his dedication and humorous kindness are still there, though they're not as evident as before.

'With regard to myself, he *does* know I exist. Jonas talks to me...includes me in what he is doing whenever he can...and...'

She was protesting too much. The look on her father's face was proof enough of that. She cut short the discussion with a subdued, 'Goodnight, Dad. I'll see you in the morning.' Then made her way upstairs to bed.

It was true what she'd said, though. Jonas did know that she existed, but in what capacity? Certainly not as a contestant for his affections. If he could get a woman like Michaela Martin, what chance would a contender like herself have?

'Forget him,' she told herself as she gazed out from her pillows into a starless sky. 'The fact that you think of him all the time when he's not there, and when he is you can't take your eyes off him, is just a blast from the past.'

If Jonas had been burning the midnight oil at the première the night before, Gemma saw that it hadn't affected his punctuality—or his efficiency. He and a senior registrar were already in Theatre when she presented herself on the unit at eight o'clock the next morning.

Eight-year-old Bobby Carstairs was the first on the list. He had been savaged by a guard dog from a local factory some time previously and had lost an ear in the attack.

The chirpy lad had been admitted the previous day for surgery which would give him a new ear.

Gemma had been present when Jonas had examined him. 'I'm going to take a piece of cartilage from his ribs,' he'd explained, 'and mould it into an ear shape. That's the first stage. The rest of the surgery consists of sewing it into the pocket of skin that was left behind when the original ear was lost.'

'How can you be sure it will match the remaining one?' she'd asked.

The question had brought forth a rare smile. 'I can't be sure, but I was always good with Plasticine when I was a kid.'

She'd smiled back at him and had been surprised to find him studying her intently. 'Why do I feel that out of all my staff you are the one that I'm getting to know the best? We haven't met before, have we?' he'd asked.

On the point of admitting that they had, Gemma had seen Peter French tuning in to the conversation and there had been no way that she'd wanted him of all people to hear that juicy titbit.

'Not that I recall,' she'd said after appearing to give the question some thought.

That had been yesterday. Today she was still obsessed with what she'd seen on television the night before—Jonas, looking incredible in evening dress, with the beautiful actress on his arm. She must be insane to think he would ever cast a glance in her direction.

However, her mirror could have told her, had she asked it, that she was just as lovely as Michaela Martin, in a fresh unspoiled sort of way, with her dark almond eyes, creamy skin and long shining hair.

And that was about the total of it. She wasn't an achiever—at the top of her profession like Jonas and the actress—but, then, they were a few years ahead of her, she reminded herself.

Jonas appeared on the unit in the middle of the afternoon and caught her having a laugh with one of the nurses. Eyeing her unsmilingly, he said, 'Would you come to my office for a moment, please, Dr Bartlett?'

The nurse rolled her eyes and turned away without

speaking, and Gemma knew that they were both thinking the same thing...that she was in trouble of some sort.

They weren't wrong.

'Take a seat,' he said abruptly as he perched himself on the corner of his desk. He waited until she was settled and went on, 'I've just had a phone call from your father.'

'Dad!' she exclaimed, gripping the arms of the chair. 'Is something wrong?'

Jonas shook his head. 'No, nothing like that.'

'What, then?'

'He rang to put me in the picture.'

Gemma could feel her cheeks warming. What did he mean?

'What picture?' she croaked with a sinking feeling at the pit of her stomach.

'A picture of me being the one who did your surgery after the car crash, which prompts me to ask why it had to be a big secret. Why didn't you admit we'd met before when I asked you yesterday?'

She swallowed hard and, ignoring his question, came up with one of her own. 'Did he say anything else?'

Jonas had eased himself off the corner of the desk and had gone to stand by the window with his back to her.

'Er...yes. He said that your feelings for me had got out of hand and would I, please, have a word with you?'

'Oh! No!' she groaned. 'How could he?'

'Don't feel bad about it, Gemma,' he said in a gentler tone. 'He seems to think that you're missing the chance of happiness with someone else because you have this...er...fixation with regard to myself.'

He was trying to let her off lightly, the junior doctor who had this embarrassing 'fixation' for him.

Her humiliation was accompanied by anger which was aimed first of all at her father for his bumbling interference in the most private part of her life. Then there was rage at herself for letting a situation such as this ever develop, and lastly, but to a lesser degree, with Jonas for telling her about Harry's phone call.

He could have kept it to himself and saved her this horrendous humiliation, she thought wretchedly, but would she have wanted to be at that sort of a disadvantage—Jonas knowing how she felt about him and not telling her?

Desperate to salvage some dignity, she said quickly, 'It was all a long time ago. I was hurt and frightened and you made me well. You were different in those days...not so grim and snappy. I was only a kid and I had a crush on you, that's all.

'My dad has got this bee in his bonnet that I won't look at anyone else because of the way I feel...felt...about you, but it's not so. For one thing I've thought for the last ten years that you were married to someone called Paula Erskine. Then I discovered that she wasn't around, but last night I saw you on TV with Michaela Martin so you are clearly involved with *someone*.'

If Jonas had taken the wind out of her sails, by informing her of her father's phone call, she had just done the same to him.

He was eyeing her, slack-jawed with amazement. 'Well! All I can say in reply is that you're jumping to conclusions, Gemma Bartlett, with regard to what you seem to think are my liaisons with your own sex. You were correct in your surmise about myself and Paula Erskine,' he went on, his face as grey and bleak as the November day outside. 'I was the gullible fool she roped in to provide a father for the child she was carrying from an affair that I knew nothing about.

'I met Paula at a hospital function and had been attracted to the daughter of one of the hospital chiefs. I was a busy surgeon, I didn't have much opportunity to look deeper and stupidly I let myself make a commitment.'

He was smiling but it was tight around the edges. 'I wasn't to know at that time that one of my young patients was interested in me, but even if I had it would have made no difference. How old were you?'

'Seventeen,' she mumbled uncomfortably.

'Exactly. Where now I am observing an attractive junior doctor, at that time I would have just seen a schoolgirl.

'Paula and I hadn't slept together before the wedding but almost immediately she announced she was pregnant, and although I felt it was a bit soon I was delighted. When the child was born at seven months she tried to persuade me, a medical man, that it was a honeymoon baby born prematurely.

'Even if I'd been gullible enough to believe her, there was one snag that she must have been praying wouldn't come up. The little one's skin wasn't the same colour as mine…or hers. Daniel's father was an Indonesian medical student who had beaten a sharp retreat back to his native land and conveniently disappeared.

'My natural exuberance, which you referred to, drained away on the day the baby was born. Needless to say there was a horrendous row and I filed for divorce shortly afterwards.'

'What happened to her?' she asked quietly.

'Paula did the same trick as her boyfriend. She disappeared after the baby was born, and as she'd shown no interest in Daniel it wasn't a surprise when she left him behind. I haven't seen her from that day to this. I neither know nor care what has happened to her.'

'And the baby?'

'Daniel lives with me.'

Gemma's mind was reeling as she said hotly, 'How could she do that to you? To me you were a god. The ward lit up when you walked in with your smiling confidence. You were kind and caring, always making us laugh.'

'And now I don't?'

'No. You don't. You've changed. But surely you're
happy now…with Michaela Martin?'

He had come to stand beside her and she was surprised
to see amusement in the brown eyes looking down into
hers.

'I'm sure you'll be surprised to hear that the beautiful
Michaela is my stepmother. My father is a well-preserved
virile, sixty-year-old, at present away on a prolonged business trip, and as she has a part in a play at a London theatre
his bride has come up from the country to stay at my place.

'Last night when you saw me on the box I was merely
doing the honours. And now that I've come clean, what are
we going to do about you?'

Gemma's mind was still whirling but the question
brought her back to earth.

'Nothing!' she snapped. 'Nothing at all! I'm furious with
my dad. He had no right to phone you.'

Jonas was shaking his head as if she was overreacting.
'It was only because he has your welfare at heart.'

Still angry, she snarled back, 'I can take care of my own
"welfare"!'

He held out a placatory hand towards her and as she
looked down on the strong capable fingers Gemma wanted
to touch them, to hold them against her cheek and tell him
that her feelings for him weren't in the past. They were
here in the embarrassing present—a present where she was
going to have to pretend that he wasn't forever in her
thoughts, because if she didn't the constraint between them
would be unbearable.

She was on her feet, ready to go, but he had something
else to say and she listened with bent head, unable to meet
his eyes.

'Before we delete this conversation from our minds, tell
me one thing, will you?'

'What?'

'I'm asking you again—why the big secret? Why didn't you want me to know I was the one who repaired your face?'

'You've only been here a few weeks,' she said lamely, 'and the opportunity hasn't arisen. That's one reason, and the other is that I hoped you might remember me without having to be prodded.'

'Hmm. Well, sorry about that, but I did say that there was something familiar about you…'

She'd had enough. All she wanted was to escape back to the ward and reality…to end this discussion which had cleared the air in some ways and complicated her life in others.

So fraught was she that the thought came to mind that maybe life with the unexciting Roger was what she needed, because being around Jonas Parry was like walking on glass.

'Off you go, then,' he was saying, 'and don't be too hard on your father. Do you want me to ring him back to confirm that I have "had a word" as he requested?'

'No!' she said with a shudder. 'I can't bear the thought of being discussed any further.'

'Don't make too much out of nothing,' he advised. Taking her capable, ringless hand in his, he said, 'The right man for you will appear one day and hopefully you'll get a better deal than I did.'

At his touch she became still. It wasn't the first time she'd felt his hands on her. He must have done it countless times when he'd been treating her all those years ago, but then she would have been anaesthetised and have known nothing about it. Whereas now she was so aware of him that it seemed incredible that he couldn't tell. The contact was light and impersonal, yet Gemma felt as if she was being burned by fire where their hands were touching.

As she pulled out of his grasp and reached blindly for the doorhandle he said casually, as if the last half-hour had been spent discussing trivialities, 'Let's get together some time. I'd like to talk to you about what we did for you all that time ago. Looking at you, I can only think I must have been inspired.'

'Thought you'd got lost,' Peter French said when she got back to the ward. 'What did Parry want you for?'

Gemma smiled. Jonas's last comment had wiped out some of the mortification her father had wished upon her.

'Nothing,' she told him with a lift to her voice.

'Huh! Expect me to believe that?' he sneered. 'You were Soames's favourite and now it looks as if it's going to be the same with this fellow.'

Gemma eyed him coolly. This man she could handle. 'That's rubbish and you know it. If the consultants single me out it's because they know that I'm keen and able. You should try it yourself some time.'

'What?'

'Showing an interest in the job you get paid for.'

The ward sister was beckoning and without giving him the chance to make further nasty comments Gemma went to see what was required of her.

Bobby Carstairs was back on the ward after his ear operation but now he wasn't chirpy at all. He'd pulled off the bulky dressing that had been placed over his ear along with the crêpe bandage that was keeping it in place and was crying that it was too tight and that it hurt.

Gemma gave the young patient her most winning smile and then turned to the sister. 'Jonas won't be pleased if he knows that the dressing has been removed. There's always a risk of infection. It will have to go back but with the bandage tied more loosely.'

The ward sister nodded but wasn't entirely convinced.

'Then it will become dislodged again, won't it,' she queried, 'if it isn't tight enough?'

Gemma shook her head. 'Not if you do it this way. Instead of wrapping the bandage tightly around the forehead, separate it, making it slacker as you do so. Then as you take it round the rest of the head bring it back into line. So that the loosened part at the front doesn't cause it to slip, fasten it at the sides with tape. Whatever happens, the dressing must stay on.' With another smile for the scowling Bobby, she said, 'You do want a new ear, don't you, Bobby?'

'Course I do,' he grumbled, 'but I don't want a headache gettin' it.'

'You won't...now,' she soothed, and left him to the nurse's ministrations.

Her father was preparing the vegetables when Gemma arrived home that evening. He looked up sheepishly when she appeared in the kitchen doorway.

'All right. I know I'm an interfering old fool,' he admitted gruffly, 'but ever since your mother died I've been concerned that if anything should happen to me, you would be completely alone. I admit that I shouldn't have rung Jonas Parry. I don't know what possessed me, but I was only thinking of your best interests. I want to see you settled before I follow your mother.'

Gemma sighed. 'If that's the case, you're going the wrong way about it, Dad. After putting me in such an embarrassing position with Jonas, I doubt I'll be able to look another man in the face...ever.'

'I just wanted him to make you realise that he lives in a different world to you. You weren't the only one who saw him on TV last night.'

'Yes, but he doesn't,' she protested. 'Michaela Martin is the woman in his father's life—not his—and as for the one he was to marry years ago, well, he did marry her, but it was over in a short space of time. So basically I'm not chasing a man who belongs to someone else, and as far as our working lives are concerned, you can't say that we belong to different worlds there.

'But you don't need to worry about me pining for Jonas any more. The fact you told him how I feel about him has put an end to all that!'

'I can't believe that I've made such a mess of things,' he said remorsefully, and because she loved him Gemma went and held him close.

'Forget it, Pops,' she told him generously. 'It wouldn't have come to anything anyway. What's for dinner? I'm starving.'

His sigh of relief came straight from the heart and he picked up the potato peeler again while Gemma took off her snug winter coat and went to lay the table.

The next day Gemma eyed Jonas warily when he came on the ward. Her embarrassment from their revealing meeting less than twenty-four hours ago was still uppermost in her mind and she was dreading that he might refer to it, but she found that there was no need to worry.

He spoke at length with Peter and the sister about a man who had been admitted the previous day for skin grafts, after being burnt some time previously in a chip-pan fire, but merely gave a brief nod in her direction.

So the fact that they'd been baring their souls to each other yesterday hadn't turned them into bosom buddies, she thought, undecided whether to be relieved or peeved.

It was two weeks later when Jonas stopped her in the staff restaurant and said, 'We never did have that chat about your time spent in my care. How about refreshing my memory one night this week at my place?'

Gemma almost dropped her tray. It was the last thing she'd been expecting when he had come alongside her in the food queue.

'Er, yes, if you wish,' she managed. 'I'm free most nights this week which makes a change. Last week would have been a different matter as I was on Casualty and never seemed to get away on time.'

'I thought I hadn't seen you around,' he commented casually. 'So, what night is it to be?'

'Tomorrow?'

'Yes. That will be fine. Give me your address and I'll pick you up.'

'No!' she said quickly. The last thing she wanted was for her father and Jonas to meet. If they did, her parent might start making something out of nothing, as she herself was doing at that moment because her heart was fluttering like a wild bird in her breast.

'I can make my own way to your flat if you'll direct me,' she suggested, and was relieved when he nodded.

'OK. Suit yourself. About seven-thirty, shall we say?' And then, as if he'd decided to rock the boat at the last minute, 'You'll be quite safe. My son will be there to chaperon us.'

'Your son?'

'Yes, mine. I have legally adopted Daniel.' The tight mask which was the trade mark of what he'd become was in position. 'Somebody had to be responsible for him and once you've met him you'll see that it isn't a chore.'

'I look forward to it,' she said gravely.

'Good. That's settled, then. Now I'll go and tag onto the end of the queue.'

Jonas's ground-floor flat in Pimlico was what Gemma had expected it to be—large and sumptuous. At first glance it looked too big for a man and a small boy, but if, as he'd already explained, his glamorous stepmother was using it as a base, maybe it wasn't that huge after all.

A pretty, blonde girl with a pouting mouth and heavily made-up eyes opened the door to her and showed no surprise on seeing her standing there.

'Hi,' she said airily. 'You Gemma Bartlett?'

'Yes,' she replied, wondering if Jonas would have the same sort of comforting explanation for the presence of this girl as he'd had for the actress.

'I'm Cheryl Martin, Michaela's younger sister,' she said, answering the question in Gemma's mind almost before it had formed. 'Do come in.'

As Gemma stepped over the threshold Jonas came striding through a door at the end of a spacious hallway with a smiling boy at his heels, and suddenly Gemma had the strangest feeling…as if it was a moment she had been waiting for subconsciously all her life.

Yet why? It wasn't as if this was the occasion of their meeting after the ten-year gap. That had occurred on the hospital corridor when a plastic toy had fallen out of her pocket, and the time they'd spent alone in his office the other day had been embarrassing rather than momentous. So why now?

Relaxed in his home surroundings, Jonas was wearing a blue cashmere sweater and grey trousers and the boy, Daniel, a Spur's football shirt with matching shorts. Although they weren't touching, Gemma could feel the loving bond between the boy and the man as if it were a tangible thing.

It was then that she knew she wanted to be a part of it…to have Jonas feel that way about her, too…and all her protests that she wasn't in love with him were shown up for the sham that they were.

As Jonas stepped forward to greet her, with his adopted son hovering by his side, the blonde girl picked up an evening bag off a nearby table and, blocking his path, kissed him lingeringly on the lips.

'Bye, Jonas, darling,' she drawled. 'See you later.' With a faint smile in Gemma's direction as she went past, she said, 'Nice to have met you.'

Gemma stifled a groan. Why was it that no sooner had the threat of one woman in his life been laid to rest than another appeared? And this one was fancy-free if the last few seconds were anything to go by.

'You've got lipstick on your mouth, Daddy,' Daniel said with a worried look in the direction of the departed Cheryl.

'Have I?' Jonas said easily. Taking a large white handkerchief from his pocket, he wiped it off with slow, deliberate movements.

'Sorry about that,' he sighed. 'My "step-aunt" is a very affectionate young woman, but I'm sure that you're not interested in the comings and goings of my household.'

He was stretching out his hand. 'Let me take your coat, and then hopefully we can settle down for an uninterrupted evening.'

'I've got a new Playstation, Dr Bartlett,' Daniel said with his dark eyes shining, 'so I'll be playing on that while you're talking to Dad.'

Jonas's adopted son was a beautiful child, she thought, observing the black waves, close cut over his head, and the smooth coffee-coloured skin against which his teeth gleamed whitely. It was no wonder that Jonas hadn't been able to part with Daniel. Wherever this Paula Erskine woman was, she was missing the joy to be had from a child such as this.

When he had settled her in a chair by the fire and placed a drink in her hand, Jonas looked at her thoughtfully.

'So, tell me about it, Gemma. What happened all those years ago?' he said.

'A friend who had just passed her test took me for a

drive and we ran into an oncoming car,' she said with economic truth. 'She was unhurt in the collision, but I suffered a fracture of the maxilla.'

He was listening intently. 'And?'

'You had difficulty in getting a clear airway after the accident and, after keeping a close watch on me, ordered a tracheostomy.'

'And?' he repeated.

'I had to have my jaws wired to bring the fractured bones into place.'

Jonas got to his feet. 'Come here,' he commanded, and when she obeyed and went to stand in front of him he took her face in his hands and began to feel it carefully with his fingertips.

She knew that as far as he was concerned the exercise was entirely professional, but for Gemma his touch on the fine scars, her lips, her high cheek-bones and on the slender stem of her throat—along with his disturbing nearness— was pushing her to the limit of self-control.

When she began to tremble his hands became still and the eyes looking down into hers lost their impersonality.

'You're shaking,' he said quietly, releasing her face. 'Am I upsetting you? Bringing back bad memories?'

She shook her head. Was this man who filled her every waking thought wearing blinkers? Maybe he wasn't.

'Or are we on different tracks?' he was asking. 'Tuned in to different sorts of chemistry? Because if that's the case maybe I ought to do something about it.'

'Such as what?' she breathed.

'This for starters.' Bending his head to hers, Jonas kissed her gently on the lips. 'That is for remembering me…for thinking well of me…and taking the new miserable me in your stride,' he said, against her quivering mouth. 'And this is for no other reason than that you are near and very desirable.'

He was kissing her again but this time the gentleness was replaced with a hungry passion that rocked her very being, and as she responded they clung together, welded by the heat of their need.

It was Jonas who had started the crazy avalanche of feeling and it was he who came to his senses first, unwrapping his arms from around her enticing slenderness, removing his lips from hers.

For her part Gemma would have stayed in his arms for ever. Hadn't she dreamt of this, longed for it? And now it was as if her feelings for the man who had changed her life all those years ago were being returned.

But she was assuming too much, and as he drew away her heart sank like lead. Even before the words left his mouth she knew what was coming, and the knowledge didn't make them any less painful.

'I must be insane,' he breathed raggedly, running a distraught hand through his thick bronze crop. 'You're a member of my staff and a junior one at that. I should be training you, guiding you, not seducing you! Your father would have a fit if he knew just how little notice I've taken of his phone call the other day.'

'For goodness' sake, Jonas,' Gemma flung back angrily. 'I wish you and my father would stop treating me as if I'm unable to manage my own affairs. I coped with the pain and trauma of a middle third fracture to my face and then went on to medical school where I also coped, and now I'm holding down a job that I find totally absorbing, so why all the fuss?'

'It's a matter of ethics,' he said flatly. 'Professional *and* sexual.'

'I see. Then I'd better go. Would you get my coat, please?'

He sighed. 'There's no call for high drama. I get enough of that from Michaela.'

'And her sister?'

He was eyeing her blankly. 'Cheryl, you mean? Yes She's into kissing, I'm afraid.'

With the memory of their own recent performance, sting ing now, rather than being measured in delight, she snapped back, 'With different degrees for different people?'

'That applies to all of us, doesn't it?' he remarked lev elly, calm now after the tempest.

As he stood at the door a few minutes later and watched Gemma's car pull away into the dark London night, Jonas' face was sombre. Gemma Bartlett was sweet and vulnera ble. If she'd been as she was now when he'd treated her injuries, who could say what might have happened? Bu she'd been just a kid and he? He'd been about to embark on the most disastrous period of his whole life, a time that had changed him for ever.

'I'm hungry, Dad. Can we go for a take-away?' Daniel' voice said suddenly from behind him, and as Jonas swiv elled to face his son the thought came, as it often had be fore, that one good thing had come from that nightmare time when he'd been married to Paula. Here beside him was his reason for living.

He supposed it wasn't surprising that tonight he was harking back to the past, what with the girl he'd treated all that time ago being a visitor to his home…and the envelope lying on his desk that held a letter from Paula's father con taining the news that she had died some weeks previously in a boating accident in the Cameroons.

Daniel had no memory of his mother so he would feel little grief. As for himself, he was sorry that her life had been cut short, but there was relief in him, too, because the threat of her ever trying to take the boy from him had been averted for all time.

CHAPTER THREE

WITH the memory of the night before like scar tissue on her heart, Gemma's expression was bleak as she drove to the hospital the next morning. If Jonas was in the market for saving faces, so would she be, she vowed. Her own!

Somehow or other she had to show him that she wasn't the pliable piece of putty he was mistaking her for. Her cheeks went hot every time she recalled the excuse he'd used to put her in her place after their melting point had been reached and then quickly returned to solidity.

The ethics of the situation were what he'd been considering, or so he'd said, when he'd put paid to her brief flight to the stars, but she didn't believe him.

He hadn't been breaking into a sweat at the thought of the ethics involved with the lingering kiss that he'd received from his stepmother's sister of all people, a kiss that had obviously caused his delightful son some concern if Daniel's expression had been anything to go by.

No. It was only his gravitation towards herself that had caused his withdrawal. But, then, she supposed it was hardly surprising. He'd already been warned by her father that she had designs on him, and when the matter had been discussed she'd only made a weak attempt to deny it.

He must have seen a trap waiting for him last night when they'd ended up in each other's arms, and he'd taken immediate steps to avoid it. But it was Jonas who'd made the first move, not her. Well, whatever was going on in his mind, he need have no further worries. From now on he would be lucky if she even looked at him.

The confrontation she'd been dreading didn't occur until

41

late in the morning, just as she and James were finishing the ward rounds of the less serious cases.

'Mr Parry has just rung from Casualty,' the ward sister said. 'He wants you both down there immediately.'

James had only been back from sick leave a week and so his introduction to the new head of plastic surgery had been very recent, but like the rest of them he was impressed and in awe of the top man's talents.

'Does Jonas Parry do private cosmetic treatments?' he asked as they waited for the lift to transport them downwards. 'For the society beauties, politicians, the acting fraternity and suchlike?'

'Not that I know of,' Gemma told him.

'Lots of these guys do, though, don't they?' he persisted. 'Making a very nice income on top of their hospital work.'

'I suppose so,' she agreed, 'but I know which part of the job Jonas would put first.'

He might be out of favour in some ways, but it was as natural as breathing for her to defend his integrity.

The man he was examining when they got to Casualty was very pale. He had been brought there with a big roller towel around his hand which was bright with blood.

'Severed thumb. Decision time,' Jonas said briefly when they went to stand by him.

'Got my hand stuck in some machinery,' the man said in a quavery voice, 'and it's whipped off my thumb.'

'Have we got it?' Gemma asked with a commiserating glance at the injured workman.

Jonas shook his head. 'No. Unfortunately. So microsurgery is out of the question. A thorough search has been made of the machinery and the surrounding area, but it looks as if it has been pulped.'

'I saw it going through the grinder,' the patient said with a shudder. 'It could have been worse, I suppose. It could have been my arm, but that's not much help at the moment.'

'The painkillers you've been given will keep your hand reasonably comfortable for a while.' Jonas told him, 'and during that time would you mind if my colleagues examine the injury, as we have to decide what we are going to do to repair the damage?'

Gemma's smile was tightly incredulous. 'We' he'd said. *We* are going to repair the damage. He was joking, of course. Neither she nor James had reached that stage in their training. Maybe Peter was up to it, but not them.

What Jonas really wanted to know was how much knowledge they had acquired with regard to this sort of situation because one day they would have to deal with it themselves. That thought had excitement and apprehension walking hand in hand.

'Dr Bartlett. What would you suggest in a situation of this sort?' Jonas asked with a muted pleasantness that made her wonder if she'd dreamt last night's incident.

She took a deep breath. 'I feel that there are a few choices.'

'And what are they?'

'A bone graft could be done from the hip or rib, trimming it to the required length and then inserting it into the stump of the metacarpal.' She turned towards the injured man. 'To use less technical terms, the skeleton of the hand. It would then have to be covered with skin from possibly the groin and positioned so that it would develop into a tube shape.'

Jonas was listening intently and when she stopped for breath he butted in. 'Would there be any sensation in the resurrected thumb?'

Gemma shook her head. 'No, but if a flap of skin was taken from the ring finger and used to cover the tip of the new thumb some degree of sensation would be restored.'

'And how successful would this method be cosmetically?'

'A crude affair,' she replied.

'Correct. So what other suggestions do you have?'

She wished he would turn his attention to James, instead of beaming in on herself all the time, but he was waiting for an answer and so was the injured man.

'Move one of the fingers across and implant it where the thumb used to be, complete with nerves, vessels and tendons, as the loss of a thumb is far more serious than that of a finger.'

'And?'

'Join the phalanx with a bone peg and wire it into position, then encase it in plaster.'

'For how long?'

She hesitated. 'Three weeks?'

Jonas nodded. 'Hmmm. That's about right. Any other suggestions?'

Was he doing this deliberately? she wondered. Putting her on the spot. Making her earn her keep. Maybe he wanted to catch her out…to make up for last night in some sort of obscure way.

'I asked if you'd any other suggestions?' he was persisting.

'Only one,' she said with a flippancy she was far from feeling. 'That you give Dr Brice a chance to air *his* knowledge.'

'In other words, you've not heard of using a toe to replace a thumb?' he asked with a chill in his voice. Without giving James the chance to get a word in edgeways, he turned to the man whose injury they'd been discussing.

'I'm going to have to assess the situation very carefully with regard to the surgery. In the meantime, you might give some thought as to whether you would prefer to have a small, manufactured, unsightly thumb, without the loss of

a finger, or whether we should deprive you of one of them
to give you back the mobility that you've lost.'

'And my toes?

'Yes, there is that. We might be able to transplant a
toe…after we've amputated it.'

The man shook his head wretchedly. 'They all sound
painful choices.'

Jonas patted him on the shoulder. 'They'll be taking you
up to the ward in a few moments. I'm told that you've
already had your hand X-rayed. When I've seen the results
I'll get back to you.' With a brief nod in the direction of
the two junior doctors he went on his way.

'Whew! I'm glad it was you in the *Mastermind* seat!'
James said as they made their way back to the wards. 'Parry
doesn't dawdle around, does he?'

'Er…no,' she agreed. 'Not in anything he does.'

As the weeks went by Gemma felt as if her visit to Jonas's
flat had been part of a dream. It was never referred to by
either of them and yet sometimes he spoke about Daniel in
a way that showed he hadn't forgotten that the two of them
were acquainted.

She frequently scanned the entertainment announcements
in the newspapers to see if Michaela Martin was still playing in the West End, and each time she saw that it was so
she wondered if Cheryl was still bestowing her kisses.

Was she staying at Jonas's apartment with her sister?
Gemma wondered. Or had she merely been a visitor that
night, like herself?

Whatever the answer, they'd both ended up doing the
same thing—kissing the man who lived there. But where
on the face of it he'd enjoyed what the pouting Cheryl had
to offer, his approach towards those melting moments with
herself had been downbeat and definite once he'd got himself in hand.

Needless to say, there had been no repeat performance
and whenever Gemma felt his inscrutable hazel gaze on her
she wondered whether the episode had been filed away under 'Do not get too familiar with junior staff'. It would be
in keeping with his excuse for cutting short the magic. Or
maybe there was another reason for it that she didn't know
about. Whatever the answer, it had obviously been an isolated occurrence.

It wasn't imagination on her part that he was more relaxed with the other female members of the hospital staff
than he was with her.

On a raw Monday morning in early December Gemma
opened her bedroom curtains to the glare of snow and the
sound of a shovel clanking on stone.

The white carpet was a surprise. The fact that her father
was already clearing the drive for her to get the car out
wasn't.

An early riser, he would have already breakfasted, and
now, warmly wrapped and with his sunken cheeks glowing
from the cold, he was down there, shovelling away.

He looked after her in his quiet, caring way and ever
since his disastrous phone call to Jonas had never referred
to his hopes for an understanding between herself and
Roger, or with anyone else for that matter. But Gemma was
well aware of what was being left unsaid, especially with
regard to her feelings for a divorced plastic surgeon with
an adopted son whose birth had been the cause of the marriage break-up.

She had hesitated about telling her father the story that
Jonas had told her about what had gone on in his life during
the months after she and her parents had left the area.

But on the assumption that if she didn't tell him someone
else eventually would, she had put him in the picture and

been dismayed that he hadn't seen Jonas's adoption of the boy in the same light as she had.

To her it had been an extension of his character...his kindness, his caring generosity. If the light appeared to have gone out of him, *that* hadn't changed, but to Harry it had been something else to make him unsuitable as the recipient of his daughter's affections.

'The fellow is divorced, living with tarty females and now you tell me that he has a son of unknown parentage,' he had spluttered angrily. 'Do you think that I want my daughter pining for somebody like that? Bringing up somebody else's child?'

'None of that matters if you love someone,' she'd told him gently.

If Jonas had a house full of other people's children it wouldn't have bothered her, not if he'd loved her. They would make babies of their own.

You're crazy, she'd told herself as her father had stomped off in what for him had been a rare moment of outrage. You're defending a man who hasn't looked at you for weeks.

When Gemma came out of the shower all had gone quiet down below, and as she towelled her hair dry she was smiling. That hadn't taken long. Dad must be on top form this morning.

Walking across to the window, she looked down onto the drive and her heart missed a beat. The silence wasn't because her father had finished the task he'd set himself. He was lying quite still in the slush with his leg trapped beneath him at an awkward angle and blood running down the side of his face.

The need to get to him was so great that when she thought about it afterwards she didn't remember throwing off the towel she was draped in and flinging on a robe or flying down the stairs two at a time.

All that registered was that one of the two men she loved more than life itself was lying injured and helpless down below.

Strangely, it was the other man who came into that category that she saw first on their arrival at the hospital's casualty department.

In the act of parking his car on the forecourt, Jonas watched in amazed alarm as Gemma got out of the ambulance, still in the white towelling robe she'd thrown on, with her feet in fluffy mules and her hair still in damp tendrils around an ashen face.

He was beside her in seconds.

'What's happened, for God's sake?' he breathed as the paramedics carefully stretchered her father out of the vehicle.

Gemma was trembling so much her teeth were chattering. Taking off his overcoat, he placed it quickly around her, saying urgently as he did so, 'You're going to get pneumonia!'

Ignoring the warning, she said hoarsely, 'Dad was clearing the snow off the drive and he's either fallen or collapsed. He's been unconscious ever since I found him.'

They were wheeling him towards the entrance and as Jonas fell in step beside her his keen gaze was raking the face of the still figure on the trolley.

Heart, maybe, he was thinking. Or a stroke…or just a straightforward fall from slipping on the ice. The injury to the head could be from any of those things.

But his main concern was for the girl squelching along beside him in her totally inadequate footwear. If anything happened to her father Gemma would be alone.

It was an ideal time for Harry's choice of a husband to step forward from where he was waiting in the wings, and grief and loneliness could cloud the most sensible of judgements.

You're galloping ahead somewhat, he told himself grimly. And why is the thought of this beautiful girl throwing herself away on someone she doesn't love getting *you* all steamed up? You've given her the brush-off on the pretext of being all wise and wonderful, so forget the imaginings and concentrate on being there for her—as a friend—when she needs you.

'Can you provide Dr Bartlett with a cup of hot, sweet tea?' he asked of a young nurse in Casualty as the paramedics wheeled Gemma's father into a cubicle. 'And something dry to put on her feet, even if it's only a pair of thick socks.'

The girl nodded obediently and went to carry out his request.

'I'm all right,' Gemma croaked protestingly as they followed the stretcher trolley into the cubicle.

'Hmm. You look it,' Jonas commented drily. 'Drink the tea when it comes, will you? And take those sopping wet mules off your feet while we see to your father.'

'I'm a doctor, too, you know!'

He sighed. 'I do know that, but at this moment you're a doctor in shock. We in the medical fraternity are no different from everyone else when it comes to *our* nearest and dearest.'

His eyes had left her bleached face. He was looking past her, and when Gemma turned she saw that the nurse had returned with a mug of steaming tea in one hand and a pair of thick bed socks in the other. As she accepted them gratefully Jonas nodded his approval.

The doctor in charge of Casualty had come hurrying to join them and his eyes widened when he saw the man and woman with the patient.

He recognised Gemma as a junior doctor employed at the hospital, and from the look of her she must have been in the bath or shower when the crisis had arisen.

Her companion, who was bending over the unconscious man, was Jonas Parry, the plastic surgeon, and where he had materialised from he would very much like to know.

In answer to his enquiring glance Gemma said, 'This is my father. He was shifting snow off the front drive and when I went down I found him lying unconscious, with blood pouring from the gash on his head. I think he'd hit the rain butt as he fell. His leg looks as if it's fractured too.'

'I think you're right,' Jonas agreed briefly and, turning to the other doctor, he said, 'What do you think? Heart attack? Stroke?'

'The paramedics have been checking him over in the ambulance and can find no signs of either,' the other man said. 'It's possible that it was just a fall but that he went down with such force that he knocked himself out completely.'

At that moment Harry gave a low, gasping sort of moan and slowly opened his eyes.

Gemma was by his side in a flash and as he focused on her blearily he murmured, 'I slipped, Gemma, girl. Where am I now? Hospital?'

'Yes, Dad,' she told him grimly.

'I'm in good hands, then.' He closed his eyes again. 'My head feels as if it's been hit by a ten-ton truck.'

'Yes, I know,' she soothed gently, 'and you've hurt your leg, too. Don't try to move it, will you?'

'I couldn't if I tried,' he admitted, and with a glance at Jonas, who was the nearest of the two doctors, he said, 'So, what's next? X-rays?'

'My colleague here is the casualty doctor,' Jonas told Harry. 'I was on the hospital forecourt when they brought you here and...'

Gemma's heart was thudding. It was typical that the two men in her life should meet under circumstances such as these. Should she let the moment pass? Wait until another opportunity presented itself for them to get acquainted?

No. The compulsion to introduce them was too strong. 'This is Jonas Parry, Dad,' she said quietly. 'As he's just said, he saw us arrive and came to my assistance.'

'Oh, aye?' her father said dubiously, gazing up at the man who had saved his daughter's face a long time ago and earned his deep gratitude. It was what he'd done to her heart that was making him less gracious than he would have been.

'We've met before,' Harry acknowledged. 'A long time ago.'

'Yes, so Gemma tells me,' Jonas said carefully, aware that it wasn't all that long ago since the man on the bed had warned him off, obliquely maybe but that was what it had been.

'Yes, well, it's good of you to have bothered about us,' the injured man said weakly, 'but I'm sure you have better things to take care of, such as those needing plastic surgery...and your household.'

Gemma was cringing at the side of the bed. Her father had no sooner regained consciousness than he was putting Jonas in his place, letting him see that as far as he was concerned the man who meant so much to her wasn't going to meet with *his* approval.

She knew it was his love for her that was behind it, and he *was* just recovering from a blow on the head, but Jonas wasn't to blame for the way she felt about him, and neither was he to blame for a selfish woman's misbehaviour.

Completely mortified, she turned to meet the eyes that held a mixture of amusement and pique in their hazel depths and said in a low voice, so that neither her father nor the curious member of the casualty team could hear, 'Do, please, forgive my father's rudeness, Jonas. If there

was any excuse for it—and there isn't—this isn't the time
or the place.

'You were here for me when I needed you, and I thank
you for it. We can manage now, and once we know the
extent of his injuries and the treatment he's going to need
I'll go home to change and be back on the ward as soon
as I can.'

Jonas's eyes were on her tangled locks, the thick socks
on her feet and the towelling robe wrapped around her hap-
hazardly.

'You're hardly dressed for public transport, or a taxi for
that matter. I'm going to go to the unit to let them know
I'm on the premises and then I'm coming back down and
when you're ready I'll take you home.'

He gave a wry smile as one of the casualty staff began
to wheel Harry towards the X-ray department. 'And if your
father sees it as infiltrating, too bad.'

As her anxious gaze followed the departing trolley,
bright colour stained her cheeks. Jonas could infiltrate her
life as much as he wanted. There was nothing she would
like better, but she had a feeling that the comment had been
merely a dry joke and at that moment she hadn't a laugh
in her.

It was midday and Gemma was still in the clothes in
which she'd arrived. No one had given her a second glance
as it wasn't unusual to see such an outfit in such a place,
and if they had done it wouldn't have registered, so concerned was she about her father.

The fracture had proved to be of the femur and an operation had been scheduled for the early evening. In the
meantime he had been admitted to Men's Surgical.

The deep cut to his head had been cleansed and stitched,
and an ECG and various other tests had shown no signs of
a heart attack or stroke. The only matter for concern in that
area was that he had been unconscious for so long, but as

there seemed to be no obvious cause he would be kept under observation in case of further developments.

On the face of it he had simply slipped on the ice, with severe consequences, and now she was ready to go home to change, before returning to be beside him when he went down to Theatre.

Jonas had been keeping check on the proceedings and was now waiting to take her home, and it was a comforting as well as a disturbing thought.

There didn't seem to be any obvious emotion at the prospect on his part and she supposed that was to be expected. He would see the exercise merely as doing a favour for a member of staff.

'Ready?' he asked as he appeared at the side of the bed.

Gemma nodded and, giving her father a last hug, told him, 'I'll be back shortly, Dad, just as soon as I've tidied myself up.'

'What is Parry waiting for?' he asked.

'Jonas is taking me home,' she said carefully, having no wish for a further dose of censure on the subject of their relationship...if it could be called that.

Her father's eyelids were drooping with exhaustion. 'Hmm, I see,' he murmured. 'Why didn't you phone Roger? He would have come for you.'

Gemma felt her face start to burn again. Jonas would have heard what he'd said. Once her father was back on his feet she would have to have serious words with him about this fixation he had regarding herself and Roger Croft. Couldn't he see that beside Jonas, Roger faded into insignificance?

As they walked down the corridor side by side, he in his smart suit and she in her skimpy attire, Gemma was working herself up to another apology for her father's behaviour, but as if he'd read her mind Jonas said levelly, 'Don't fret about your father's aversion to me. He sees me as the big bad wolf out to do mischief to his little ewe lamb, doesn't he?'

'Something like that,' she mumbled, and then with a grave sincerity he found totally appealing, she added, 'I've told him in no uncertain terms that he's wrong, but...'

Jonas's smile was mirthless. 'Give a dog a bad name?'

'To do that would be completely unfair. You haven't done anything to deserve it,' she protested.

'It's the packaging he doesn't like, isn't it?' he asked with a sardonic lift of the eyebrows. 'The divorced man with a motherless child? Then there are the women in my life. But I've explained that Michaela belongs to my father, and Cheryl...'

'Yes. Who does *she* belong to?'

He grinned and for a moment there was a glimpse of the laughing charmer of long ago. 'Good question, but I'll have to give it some thought.'

When they got to the house Jonas came round to the passenger side of the car, and as she swung her legs across to get out he put out a restraining hand.

'Stay where you are,' he ordered. 'You can't walk across all this slush in those socks.'

Stooping low, he placed an arm beneath her and lifted her carefully out of the car. When he straightened up Gemma found herself cradled in his arms.

It was an unbelievable moment. There was wonder in the dark velvet of the eyes looking up into his, but incredibly she spoilt it with a mundane comment.

'The neighbours will wonder what's going on.'

Jonas laughed. 'They'll be convinced I'm going to seduce you. Especially as you're only half-dressed already.'

Gemma was fishing in the pocket of her robe for the door key. Joining in his laughter, she said, 'I'd have to take my socks off first.'

He laughed again. She could feel it rumbling deep in his

chest, and when they went through the open door into the hallway he didn't put her down. Instead he stood, looking into her face.

As their eyes locked the mirth left them and Jonas said, 'I wish you *had* been grown up when we knew each other before. I wouldn't have been able to resist you.'

'Even with my battered face?' she questioned softly.

'Even with that,' he breathed, with his eyes on the smooth rise of her breasts where the robe had swung open at the top.

'And can you resist me *now*?' she asked recklessly, heedless that she might be laying herself open to hurt.

'At this moment, no,' he murmured as his lips went to the hollow of her throat. 'Tomorrow maybe, but not now.'

Gemma had become still in his arms, and as he became aware of it Jonas lifted his head.

'What is it?' he asked when he saw the mutinous light in her eyes. 'What have I done?'

'Nothing. You haven't *done* anything.'

'So it's what I've said?'

'Yes. You want me today…but not tomorrow. In other words, the girl who has this feeling for you is ready and available…so why not toss her a crumb? Put me down, please, Jonas.'

He did so, with a face as implacable as her own. 'Pity your father isn't here to see you put me in my place,' he said flatly. 'It would have made his day.' And on that cold comment he marched past her and out into the bleak December weather.

Her father's fall on the snow-covered driveway had resulted in a fracture of the neck of the femur, and as the bone ends had been displaced an operation was necessary.

Bearing in mind what the X-rays had shown, the orthopaedic surgeon was going to realign the bone ends and then fix them into position with metal plates and screws.

In such cases the patient was able to move knee and hip almost immediately after surgery but would also need bed rest for a few weeks to prevent any jarring of the bones which might delay healing.

As Gemma sat waiting for Harry to come back from Theatre, one of the hospital's social workers sought her out and her first question was, 'How are you going to cope when your father comes home?'

'I don't know,' she said dejectedly.

It had been a depressing day in more ways than one, and at that moment important decisions were the last thing she felt like facing up to.

However, it appeared that someone else was willing to make them for her...if she was agreeable.

'We can keep your father hospitalised for the next few weeks,' the social worker suggested, 'as you are employed here at the hospital and have no one to fall back on to nurse him at home.'

Gemma eyed her in surprise. 'Have we got the beds?'

'At the moment...yes. However, as we both know, that could change at any time, but unless there's an emergency I think we can manage.'

The woman smiled. 'You'll have the best of both worlds, Dr Bartlett—the knowledge that your father is being well cared for and the opportunity to see him whenever you have a minute to spare during the day.'

'That will be marvellous!' she enthused. 'If you can set it up for me I'll be really grateful.'

'Consider it done,' she was told. 'Mr Parry, the plastic surgeon, rang me this afternoon and told me that you might have a problem if your father was sent home.'

Gemma stared at her. 'Jonas Parry has been on to you?'

'Mmm. You seem to have friends in high places.'

She managed a smile. 'He's my boss. I work with him on the unit.'

'Lucky you,' the social worker said. 'I wish he was *my* boss, but you don't have to explain, you know. I'm merely doing my job, and by doing so I'm giving you the chance to do yours.' She got up to go. 'I hope that the operation has been successful when they bring him back to you.'

'Thanks,' Gemma murmured, still dumbstruck to find that Jonas had taken the trouble to mention her problem to the relevant department after their frigid parting earlier.

CHAPTER FOUR

HER father was back from Theatre and Gemma was seated beside his bed in a dimly lit side ward, waiting for him to come round.

The orthopaedic surgeon had been to see her and had given an assurance that the surgery had gone as planned. The fractured femur had been repaired, the bone ends re-aligned, and, for the rest, nature would take its course.

As she looked down at his pale face the stitches in the gash on his head were a grim reminder of the morning's trauma. It was a day that she wasn't going to forget in a hurry, for more reasons than one.

The two men she cared for had figured in it largely. One of them was helpless and injured due to an accident, and the other? He had been there in different guises—first as the supportive colleague, then as the caring friend and lastly as the lover, or he would have been if she hadn't come to her senses.

Instead, they had parted with all the caring friendship blotted out by her hurt at being used, and she wondered just how Jonas would act when next she saw him.

She was about to find out. As her father lay still, partly comatose after the anaesthetic, a shadow fell across her, and when she looked up her mouth went dry. Jonas was there with Daniel just a step behind.

'How is he?' Jonas asked without any formal greeting.

'Still not quite with us,' she told him, stating the obvious, 'but from what I've been told the operation was a success.'

Her glance went to the boy, standing uncertainly beside the man, and she said gently, 'How nice to see you, Daniel.'

58

He shuffled uncomfortably, but he met her eyes squarely enough as he said, 'Dad said would I like to come with him...and I said yes. When you came to the apartment that night I was going to show you my Playstation...but you'd gone.'

'Yes, I know,' she said apologetically, and without looking at the tall figure beside him. 'Something cropped up and I had to leave.'

'Maybe you could see it another time?'

'Yes. I'd like that.'

She would. It would be nice to get to know Jonas's son, but at the moment the chances were slim, though she couldn't tell the boy that.

She couldn't say, I don't think I'm likely to get another invitation—because she wasn't, was she? Not after what had happened between his father and herself earlier.

But it seemed as if Jonas's mind was on another track. 'Did the social worker come to see you?' he asked flatly.

She smiled and it lit up her pale face. 'Yes. Thanks for the thought. They're going to keep Dad in for as long as they can.'

He nodded. 'Good.' With a sardonic smile, he added, 'Not all my thoughts are self-motivated.'

'I never said they were.'

'No?'

Daniel was watching them with a worried frown and Gemma was immediately contrite. Youngsters soon picked up on atmosphere. She and Jonas had no right to bicker in front of him. Quickly changing the subject, she asked, 'Where are you off to when you leave here? Anywhere nice?'

The boy's face cleared. 'Ten-pin bowling. Would you like to come with us?'

Her smile was back. The implications of her father's ac-

cident were not immediately obvious to a nine-year-old, but
his father was tuned in, needless to say.

'Dr Bartlett has to stay with her father,' he told his son,
'and we'd better be going. He might have a relapse if he
sees us hovering when he awakes.'

'That was an unkind thing to say,' she said in a low
voice.

'True, nevertheless.'

'It's what I think of you that counts.'

'And we know what that is, don't we?'

'Do we?'

They were doing it again in front of the boy. Verbal
sparring. She didn't want them to part in the same mood
as they had earlier.

As Jonas turned to go she reached out and took his arm.
His face softened, but as if the meddling fates still had a
few tricks up their sleeves the door opened at that moment
and Roger Croft stood there, alarm and concern stamped
all over his face.

'I've only just heard, Gemma,' he said quickly. 'How is
Harry?'

Jonas moved out of her grasp and with a brief nod to the
newcomer he shepherded Daniel towards the door. They
are going, she thought despondently. How I wish they
weren't.

At their departure Gemma slumped down onto the chair
at the side of the bed. Misunderstanding her dejection,
Roger put a comforting arm around her.

Feeling lost and very tired, she laid her head against his
chest and immediately wished she hadn't when Jonas's
voice said from the doorway, 'Sorry to interrupt. I've put
my car keys down somewhere.'

'Are these they?' Roger asked, keeping his arm in position as he reached out for a bunch of keys on the locker.

'Yes, thanks.' The reply was clipped, and with a brief

nod in her direction Jonas made his exit for a second time, leaving her to wonder if they would ever get it right.

'Who was that?' Roger asked.

'Jonas Parry, the plastic surgeon.'

'The fellow you work with?'

'Yes, part of the time.'

'Had he been visiting your father?'

Gemma nodded. 'Yes, Jonas has been very supportive.'

She was aware that she sounded stilted but she could hardly tell Roger that Jonas had been the only person she had wanted with her during the last few worrying hours.

There was something else that she couldn't tell Roger either—that Jonas had held her close for a delightful fragment of time, and had then spoilt it by letting her see that had been all it was, just a quick moment of passion with no follow-ups.

Roger was eyeing her warily, waiting for her to elaborate on Jonas's support. With a feeling that she was gabbling, Gemma said, 'He stayed with me when we brought Dad in after the accident and he rang Social Services on my behalf. They are going to keep Dad hospitalised for as long as they can because there would be no one to nurse him at home.'

Roger was frowning. 'What about you? You could take unpaid leave.'

'Yes, I suppose I could, but we do have to live. I'm the only wage-earner.'

'I suppose that's true,' he agreed reluctantly, and then went on, to her absolute amazement, 'I wouldn't expect you to work if you married me.'

Gemma's eyes went to her father's still face. Between them he and Roger would have her hemmed in. If she'd had any doubts about the unimaginative young GP, they had just increased a hundredfold.

Only Jonas had seen the problem through her eyes and the thought brought a lump to her throat. Whatever else there was about him that was different, his kindness and caring towards others hadn't changed. What a pity that she was just another needy soul as far as he was concerned. Why couldn't he love her as much as she loved him?

'Did you hear what I said?' Roger asked with the frown still creasing his brow.

'Er…yes. Was it supposed to be a proposal?'

'Yes, although I'm afraid that it just slipped out. This is hardly the right moment, is it?'

'No, it isn't,' she agreed in level tones, 'but I might as well tell you, there won't ever be a right moment, Roger. I'm sorry, but I don't love you.'

He had gone to stand by the window and now he swung round to face her.

'It's Parry, isn't it? Your father told me you have a long-standing crush on him.'

There was anger in her now, searing white hot. 'How dare you patronise me?' she flared. 'At twenty-seven I'd say I was a bit long in the tooth for girlish crushes, and if I wasn't it has nothing to do with you…or Dad for that matter. He has no right to discuss me with you.'

She was in full spate with more to come, but her tactless suitor was saved as Harry Bartlett began to stir. Because they both cared deeply for him all other matters were put to one side in the relief of having him back in their world.

At the bowling alley Jonas tried to put to the back of his mind the vision of Gemma's dark head cradled against the chest of the young GP.

He and Daniel had barely had time to get through the door before she'd been in his arms, he kept thinking irritably.

But what was wrong with that? They were both free agents and her father had set his heart on it. Yet Jonas knew she had a mind of her own. It had been very much in evidence earlier when he'd almost succumbed to the attraction that he was trying so hard to ignore.

If his mind wasn't on the game, Daniel's was. He was pulling at his sleeve and asking, 'Did you hear what I said, Dad? It's your turn.'

He smiled down at the boy. He knew where he was with this one. Daniel was a constant source of joy. Happy and uncomplicated, his adopted son was everything he would have wanted in a child of his own. But always at the back of his mind was the question of whether a woman he loved would accept someone else's child as easily as he had?

Cheryl got on all right with Daniel but women like her needed to be the centre of attention. They didn't like having to compete with a child...and Daniel was wary of her. Jonas could tell by the way he looked at her.

Two things brought a smile to Harry Bartlett's face as he surfaced from the anaesthetic in the small side ward. One was the knowledge that the operation was behind him, and the other was the sight of his two favourite people at his bedside.

His happiness would not have been so complete if he'd known that his daughter had just turned down his friend in no uncertain terms, but neither she nor Roger were going to upset him at that moment, and once the nurses had settled him for the night they left together, only to separate outside the hospital in strained silence, each making their own way to their cars.

Driving home, Gemma's only remaining emotion was relief that the horrendous day was drawing to a close. It seemed like a thousand years since she'd looked down onto the drive and seen her father lying there.

Since then she'd been propositioned, or at least she would have been if she hadn't let Jonas see that she was no walk-over...and she'd been proposed to.

Each experience had been disturbing in its own way—the first because it would have been so easy to have let the roller-coaster of passion she and Jonas had been on pursue its way, and the second because of the fury she'd felt at Roger and her father for taking her so for granted.

But wasn't that what Jonas had been guilty of, too? He'd been informed that she had feelings for him, so had he decided to take advantage of the fact?

Yet he didn't need to, did he? He might be a low-key version of the man she'd known before, but he wasn't any less desirable. With his looks, style and reputation in the medical world, he could have any woman he chose. He'd probably had a good laugh at the presumption of a mere junior doctor thinking he was seriously attracted to her.

The next morning Gemma had herself in hand. A good night's sleep, which was more than she'd expected, had recharged her batteries and she was ready for the day ahead, a day that would be spent on the unit and visiting her father whenever the chance presented itself.

While she had been absent from the ward, James Brice, her fellow trainee, and Peter French, the registrar, had dealt with the admission of a teenage girl with facial fractures.

When Gemma read the case notes on Sally Graham she felt her nerve ends tighten. They were similar to the injuries she'd sustained herself all those years ago, in this instance a middle third fracture of the face, including the maxilla, zygomas and nasal bones, and some displacement of the teeth.

'Has Jonas seen her?' That was the first thing she said.

'Yes. He'll be operating shortly,' Peter replied with a degree of concern that was more than he usually showed, and Gemma wondered if it was because the young accident victim was the same age as his own daughter.

'When the kid was brought into Casualty yesterday she

was in a bad way,' he went on. 'By the time the paramedics got to her at the scene of the accident she was unconscious, had intra-oral bleeding and no control of the tongue due to the looseness of a fractured jaw.'

'If they hadn't pulled her tongue forward and cleared her mouth of loose teeth and blood she would have died from an airway obstruction.'

James was nodding in confirmation and added, 'The poor girl is in a terrible state with the pain and the horror of what she's done to her face. She's sedated at the moment but she has weeks of problems ahead.'

Tell me about it, Gemma thought bleakly. Who knew better than she?

'What sort of an accident was it?' she questioned.

'She was pillion passenger on the motorbike of some tearaway,' Peter said cuttingly. 'The lad escaped without injury and the girl got it all.'

'Has Jonas had a chance to talk to her?' she asked.

James shook his head. 'Not really. When she was brought in she was in no fit state to talk to anyone.'

'Why? Are you expecting him to wave a magic wand?' the sardonic registrar chipped in.

'Something like that. He did it for me.'

The two men stared at her. 'Work that one out,' she told them with an enigmatic smile.

Gemma had already been to see her father and had found that he'd had a reasonable night under the circumstances.

'I believe they're going to keep me in for a while to give the bones the chance to heal,' he'd said.

She'd nodded, looking at him anxiously. 'Don't worry, Gemma. That's fine by me,' he'd assured her. 'I don't want you running yourself into the ground, looking after me and doing your job at the same time.'

'Roger seemed to think that I should forget about my work here and take unpaid leave,' she'd told him.

He'd shaken his white thatch firmly. 'No need for you to do that. He has this thing about women being in the home, which does him credit, but in this instance I feel we're doing the right thing. Just as long as the hospital has a bed for me.'

She had stifled a sigh. If Roger Croft had said that black had been white, her father would have said it was feasible. That thought had been followed by the impulse to tell him about his GP friend's surprising proposal of marriage.

'And what did you say?' he asked immediately.

'What do you think?' she parried.

'Yes?' he said hopefully.

She shook her head. 'You know better than that, Dad. I told him no chance...ever.'

It was Harry's turn to sigh. 'So it's still your plastic surgeon?'

'Yes, but you don't need to panic. Apart from the odd vibe, there's nothing between us. Jonas isn't going to fall into my arms, protesting undying love.'

'That doesn't mean that it won't happen the other way round,' he grunted, and when a nurse loomed up with pain-killers Gemma left him to her ministrations, thinking as she did so that her father didn't give up easily when he'd set his heart on something.

But, then, neither did she. Perhaps a more positive approach was needed if she were ever to get Jonas to see her as anything but a clinging vine from long ago.

With that thought strong within her she greeted him with a warmth that made his eyebrows shoot upwards when he appeared on the ward in the late morning, but that was the only effect it had on him.

There was a chill in his manner as he asked, 'How's your father this morning?'

'Not too bad physically,' she replied.

'And mentally?'

'Somewhat surprised...and miffed.'

'And why would that be?'

Gemma hadn't forgotten Jonas's expression when he'd come back for his car keys and seen her nestling against Roger. Would he believe her if she told him the truth?

'I told him that Roger Croft had asked me to marry him and I'd said no.'

Dark brows shot upwards again. 'Well! That makes two of us who're surprised. You both looked very...attached when I came back for my keys.'

'That was merely a moment of intense weariness on my part, combined with longing.'

'Longing for what?'

'A carefree evening at the bowling alley, maybe?'

'Now you're being flippant,' he growled.

'I was never more serious.'

'What? In refusing the GP's proposal? Or going to the bowling alley?'

'Both.'

'Really? In that case we'll have to see what we can do about it.'

Gemma could see Peter looming, accompanied by the ward sister. She turned away. Just when their conversation was getting interesting an interruption was imminent.

But Jonas took her arm and kept her there. 'Don't go. Have they told you about the girl who came in yesterday with similar injuries to the ones you received?'

'Yes,' she said quietly. 'I went to have a word with her but she was sedated. She looks awful.'

'Mmm,' he agreed. 'She does. I thought that a chat with you might cheer her up when she sees how you came through your ordeal.'

'Yes, of course I'll talk to her. It will be a comfort to her to know that the same miracle-worker is going to operate on her.'

The Jonas of long ago would have made a laughing disclaimer at the title, but he wasn't around any more, was he? He'd been replaced by someone whose light had been dimmed, and as if to prove it he said sombrely, 'I'm no miracle-worker, Gemma. I just do my best with the skills that I have and am thankful. If my personal life were as gratifying as my professional then I might have something to boast about.'

'You have Daniel who's a lovely child.'

'You think so?' Was there a wistfulness about the question?

The other members of staff were about to join them. 'Of course,' she said quickly. 'Who wouldn't?'

'Sally Graham is awake,' Peter said with a curious glance at the junior doctor and the consultant.

'Right. I'll go and have a word with her,' Gemma said.

'Tell her that I'll be along myself shortly,' Jonas called after her.

The girl propped up against the pillows in a sitting position could have been herself all those years ago. Her face was very swollen but with a flattened appearance due to the fracturing of the nasal bones and the displacement of the maxilla.

She looked ill and very weary and Gemma guessed that there was nothing she would like more than to be able to lie flat, but the upright position was to help reduce the swelling and, more importantly, to assist in keeping an airway open.

A nurse had just left, after dealing with the deep lacerations on her face with an antiseptic solution, and it brought back painful memories to the young doctor of how they had virtually needed to scrub her face to remove the dirt and grit that had entered the wounds.

Similar procedures would need to be carried out in this case, too, as any grime left would leave black tattoo-like marks when the healing process was completed and by that time it would be impossible to remove them.

'I know that it's difficult for you to talk, Sally,' Gemma said gently as the girl looked at her with tear-filled eyes, 'but you can listen, can't you?'

Sally nodded in lethargic misery.

'I know what you're going through because the same thing happened to me,' Gemma said softly.

The girls reddened eyes widened.

'Yes, it did,' she assured her patient, 'and I thought I'd never look pretty again...' Gemma's smile was full of re-assurance. 'And Jonas Parry, who is one of the country's top plastic surgeons, is going to operate on you.'

She paused, to give what she had to say next the required effect before she added, 'The same as he did on me.'

As the girl's battered face brightened, Gemma continued, 'Luck may not have been on your side when you came off the bike, but it is now. You only need to look at me to realise that.'

A footstep behind had her turning swiftly with colour rising in her cheeks. Had Jonas heard her singing his praises? she wondered. What if he had?

But she didn't want him to see herself as still in the worshipping mould of long ago. She was a grown woman now, a doctor in her own right. She might be trailing behind in experience and have fewer years of health care below her belt due to her youth, but she hoped that one day she, too, might command the same respect that was given to Jonas.

And where would he be when that time came? Married to the pert blonde who had kissed him so thoroughly that night at his apartment? Or to some other dishy contender for the title of the second Mrs Parry? If that ever did come about she hoped that he would have the sense to choose someone who would love and cherish his delightful son.

His voice broke into her thoughts, cool and critical.

'I'm about to explain to Sally what I intend to do when I have her in Theatre, Dr Bartlett. If you could bring your attention to bear on the matter, it will save me having to go through it all again for your benefit.'

If her cheeks had been hot before, they were burning now—with mortification. She had let his nearness distract her from the needs of a patient—in this instance the fearful young victim of a motorcycle accident—and it wouldn't do.

The job came first and her private life second, what there was of it.

'I'm sorry, sir,' she said meekly, with an anything but humble yearning to tell him that he was the cause of her momentary aberration.

There was a question in his eyes. Was he wondering why this junior doctor who was usually so tuned in to all that was going on, wasn't up to her usual form?

His expression changed, as if he'd found his own answer, and Gemma thought he had decided she was suffering from the aftermath of the previous day's trauma, which was perhaps just as well.

If Jonas should ever think that working together was affecting her performance he might have her moved, and that would be unbearable.

'There has been no sign of cerebrospinal fluid from the nostrils,' he said, as if he, too, was having to bring his thoughts into line, 'indicating damage to the base of the skull. That's one thing you don't have to worry about, Sally.'

The smile he had for the injured girl was warm and reassuring and Gemma was taken back in time. Jonas might have lost some of his exuberance but his awareness of the fears and pain of his patients wasn't any less.

'But there are other concerns that I must attend to,' he

went on, 'and I have to tell you what they are as there is no way I can avoid causing you some pain and discomfort.

'Later today I'm going to have you taken to Theatre where I will manipulate the fractured bones in your face. Once I have done that it will be a matter of getting your teeth and jaw into line.

'A few of your teeth were lost in the accident, but Orthodontics will sort that out at a later date. The urgency at the moment is to realign the remainder, which will require the wiring of your jaws for an approximate period of six weeks.'

There was horror in the girl's eyes and Gemma thought that this was just like her own experience. She'd never forgotten how scared she'd been when they'd wired her jaws, and it was this same man who had made it endurable with his bouncy, caring confidence.

Jonas's voice was gentle as he went on to explain, 'You will be fed on liquids, Sally, and the nursing staff will be around at all times to make sure that you experience no problems. Everything will be done to make you as comfortable as possible... And remember this, my dear, a few weeks' discomfort will be worth having your pretty face back for the rest of your life.'

She nodded glumly and he turned away, telling Gemma in a low voice, 'You'll probably remember from your own experience that in this sort of case there must always be suction apparatus by the bedside and a tray with wire-cutters, screwdriver and spanner for emergency release of the wires should it be necessary.'

Her smile was grim. 'How could I possibly forget?'

'Exactly,' he agreed. 'Sally is fortunate in one sense. She will have you before her all the time she is suffering—a beautiful example of what plastic surgery can do for an injured face.'

Gemma felt her heart leap. Jonas thought her 'beautiful'.

He'd said something like that before…to the effect that he must have been inspired when he'd repaired her face.

To be told that she was 'beautiful' was a compliment that every woman craved to hear from the man in her life, she told herself chidingly, but the compliment could be paid for different reasons. It didn't necessarily mean that the bestower of it was ablaze with love for her.

It could have been said in the light of a confidence-booster. Or in Jonas's case as a compliment to his expertise. Or maybe because he was so memorable himself that he could afford to be generous to a junior doctor who was on the perimeter of his life.

Her mind zoomed back to those moments when he'd held her in his arms in the hallway of her home the previous day and had blotted out the joy of knowing he desired her by telling her that he mightn't feel the same the next time they met.

Don't start reading into a casual remark something that isn't there, she warned her treacherous heart as he moved on to a bed in the corner where a toddler was being treated for scalding. Just because Roger is panting for your attentions it doesn't follow that Jonas will ever do the same.

It was seven o'clock by the time she got off the ward and Gemma went straight to see her father. He was much more perky than he'd been earlier in the day and she hid a smile as he recounted every happening from the moment she'd left him.

He was highly pleased to have been seen by the orthopaedic surgeon who had operated on him and who was now offering an optimistic prognosis.

Harry had also had a visit from their young neighbours and a brief chat with Roger, who had called in while on his rounds.

'You've upset him,' he said gruffly. 'Turning him down flat like you did.'

'Hard lines,' she said unsympathetically. 'Roger shouldn't have taken me for granted, and in any case was I likely to be interested in a marriage proposal with you only seconds out of the operating theatre?'

Gemma was aware that the comment wasn't exactly fair. She'd been ready enough to melt when Jonas had touched her only a short time after her father had gone to Theatre, but there was a difference, wasn't there? She loved the man. For better or worse, she loved Jonas Parry.

Her father gave a reluctant chuckle. 'Yes, perhaps his timing wasn't too good. You might be more interested another time, maybe?'

'No. Never!'

He sighed, but his gloom was only momentary. The hospital chaplain had appeared in the doorway of the small ward and was suggesting a game of chess.

Clearly Harry was finding being hospitalised more interesting than pottering around the house all day on his own in spite of his injuries, Gemma thought as she went home to prepare her solitary evening meal with an easier mind than she would have expected.

It transpired that it wasn't to be a solitary occasion after all. Jonas flagged her down as she was leaving the hospital car park, and when she wound down the car window he said, 'Are you going to be eating alone?'

Gemma eyed him in surprise. What was coming next?

'Yes,' she answered briefly.

'You're not entertaining your GP friend, then?'

'Roger? No, certainly not. I'm too frazzled to entertain anyone.'

'How about coming to McDonald's with Daniel and myself, then? I've promised him that we'll eat there tonight.'

Gemma wanted to laugh. If he'd suggested a candlelit

supper in some exclusive restaurant she would have had to think about what might come of it and whether she was being used again, but this casual invitation was just what she needed. No cooking and washing-up for one thing and the company of a likeable small boy and his father in a fast food outlet.

'Pick you up in half an hour?' Jonas suggested, taking it for granted that she was going to accept.

She might have been irritated in other circumstances but, accepting that he'd read her mind rightly, she replied, 'Make it forty-five minutes and you have a deal.'

'Fine,' he said smoothly, and, stepping back, gave a dismissive wave as she drove off.

CHAPTER FIVE

IT TOOK all of the forty-five minutes Gemma had requested to drive home, change out of the crisp cotton shirt and tailored skirt she'd worn while on duty, have a quick shower and emerge in jeans, a low-necked, white top and trainers.

A critical glance in the mirror with only seconds to spare revealed a slender, dark-haired woman with brown shoulder-length hair held back by two gold slides, wide hazel eyes, and a generous curving mouth.

It *was* a beautiful face but at that moment it didn't register as such. Gemma thought she looked white and tired after the previous day's happenings. It would be an early night for her once the impromptu dinner had run its course.

As Jonas's car pulled up on the drive the phone rang and she frowned, praying that she wasn't being called back to the hospital. However, it was Roger's voice at the other end, asking how Harry was.

'Dad's doing fine,' she told him stiffly. He was the last person she wanted to be talking to, but she had to respect his affection for her father.

'I saw him briefly this morning,' he said with equal constraint, 'but couldn't stay long as I was on my rounds. I thought I'd call in later tonight. Will you be there?'

Gemma's frown deepened. What was that supposed to mean? Was he hoping she would be? Or was he hoping she wouldn't?

Jonas was sounding the car horn down below. Talking to Roger Croft wasn't what she wanted to be doing.

'No. I'm not going back to the hospital again,' she said

briefly as she eyed the outline of the boy and the man inside the vehicle. 'I'm going out for a meal and then intend on having an early night. Dad was quite chirpy when I left him earlier and I'll visit him first thing in the morning.'

'Who are you eating out with?' he asked.

Puzzled that she wasn't putting in an appearance, Jonas was getting out of the car. Impatient at the pedantic GP's inquisition, she said irritably, 'Mind your own business, Roger!'

At that she replaced the receiver with a decisive click and ran down the stairs.

'Everything all right?' Jonas questioned as she opened the door to him.

Her cheeks flushed and eyes bright with annoyance, she nodded. 'Yes. Roger phoned just as you were pulling into the drive.'

'And?'

'What?'

'Did he have a better offer?'

'Than what?'

'McDonald's.'

Gemma was tempted to tell him that if he, Jonas, had invited her to share greasy chips at a mobile refreshment bar or a stale sandwich on a park bench, it would still have been a better offer than anything Roger could have come up with, but instead she said lightly, 'Offers weren't on the menu. He wanted to know if I was going back to see Dad tonight.'

'And are you? I'll run you there once we've eaten, if you like.'

She shook her head. 'No, thanks just the same, Jonas. Dad won't be expecting to see me again today. I've checked on his condition and they're happy about it, so I haven't any worries about him at the moment.'

As they walked to the car he said, 'Is Croft intending to go to see him?'

'Yes,' she said briefly.

'And he was hoping you'd be there?'

'I don't know,' she told him evasively. 'Maybe. But do we have to talk about him?'

He smiled and it lit up the dark mirrors of his eyes. 'No, we do not!'

Daniel was seated in the back of the car, and when Jonas opened the front passenger door she said, 'I'll sit in the back with Daniel. It will give us the chance to get to know each other.'

He shrugged. 'Whatever you wish.' And with a laughing glance at his son, 'No telling Dr Bartlett all my bad habits, Danny boy.'

The boy's answering laughter had an embarrassed shyness with it and she said reassuringly, 'Forget the Dr Bartlett, Daniel. My name is Gemma. OK?'

'Yes,' he acknowledged.

'And so is McDonald's your favourite place to eat?' she asked.

Daniel nodded. 'Yes. When we dine out with my step-grandma we go to very grand places, but Dad knows what I like best.'

'You mean Michaela Martin?'

'Yes, she's married to my grandad, but she isn't much older than you, Dr Bart—er, Gemma,' he said, correcting himself.

'Michaela is quite a lot older than Gemma,' Jonas said over his shoulder in amused reproof. 'Cheryl is more in your age group,' he commented, eyeing her in the rear-view mirror.

Gemma would have liked to have pointed out that the kissy-kissy, blonde sister of his father's wife had appeared to be light years ahead of her in some things, but there was no way she wanted the worried frown to return that Daniel had displayed once before when she and Jonas had been exchanging words.

Instead, she changed the subject and asked with engaging friendliness, 'What have you been doing today, Daniel? School?'

He sighed as if the mere mention of the word was like a heavy burden upon him.

'Yes. Worse luck. I can't wait for Christmas to come, Gemma, so that I can play with my computer and get up when I want, instead of having to be ready for Dad to drop me off at school on his way to the hospital.'

She smiled. 'Lie-ins and play…no wonder you can't wait and…' To Jonas who was tuned in to their conversation, but making no comments, she said, 'I can't believe that Christmas is so near. It creeps up on one, doesn't it?'

'It does indeed,' he agreed. 'What plans have you made?'

That question was soon answered.

'None.'

He half turned in surprise. 'None! I don't believe it.'

'It's true. James is working on Christmas Day—poor guy—and I'm down for Boxing Day so I can't go far, and Dad's accident doesn't simplify matters. He'll need me around as much as possible as he's bound to be less than his usual self.'

Jonas had stopped the car in a city car park, close by where they were to eat, and as he locked the doors he said casually, 'It all sounds very forlorn. Spend it with us…Cinderella.'

The slender, dark-eyed doctor and the olive-skinned boy were looking at him in some surprise, and with the same air of nonchalance he went on in way of explanation, 'We're out on a limb, too. Nowhere to go and no one to go with if we had.'

By this time Gemma was positively goggling at him. The

keeper of paradise was opening the gates and beckoning her inside, but he'd forgotten something, hadn't he?

She'd just said that she would be looking after her father over Christmas—and wasn't Jonas the last person Harry would want to spend it with, presuming that he'd been included in the invitation?

If the bumptious Roger had been issuing it there would be no holding him back, but her father still thought that her feelings for Jonas were a continuing infatuation from long ago. He just couldn't accept that she had found the man she wanted to spend the rest of her life with, and she had a feeling that were Jonas to become aware of that fact, too, his acceptance of it would be just as hard to come by.

'I can't,' she told him, breathing hard. 'Haven't I just said that I'll be taking care of Dad? Need I say more?'

Daniel was forging ahead of them. Looking over his shoulder with the gaze of the hungry young. They began to walk faster.

'No. I suppose not... But I thought you understood that I would be expecting him to come with you.' Jonas said.

She shook her head. 'No way. He would be singing Roger's praises all the time.'

His face had a closed-up sort of look as he enquired, 'So you haven't made any arrangements with your father's favourite in the matrimonial stakes?'

It would have been simple to have said, No! Certainly not. But for some perverse reason she didn't. Instead she told him, 'Roger always spends Christmas with relatives in the Isle of Man.'

It wasn't a lie—the absolute truth, in fact. He did. But she didn't go on to inform Jonas that for the two previous years he'd invited them to go with him.

Her father would have accepted like a shot but, seeing the net drawing closer, Gemma had refused, and as Harry wouldn't hear of leaving her alone over Christmas they had stayed put.

And now the season was approaching again and the fact was being brought home to her once more that she and her father were isolated in their own little world.

What joy it would be to spend Christmas with Jonas and Daniel...and her dad, if he would accept the invitation in the right frame of mind.

To see Daniel on Christmas morning, opening his gifts! Had he rumbled the Santa Claus myth yet? she wondered. Or was he hanging onto the magic of it for as long as he could?

As they were being served Daniel said with a grin, 'When Grandad and Michaela brought me here once she wanted to know where the plates were.'

Gemma laughed back at him. 'And what does Cheryl say when she comes here?'

His face straightened and she knew immediately that he had reservations about the actress's sister.

'Nothing. She's never been. I don't go with them when Dad takes her for a meal.'

Jonas was out of earshot, striding ahead of them with a loaded tray.

'Is that because you're not invited, or because you don't want to go?' she asked softly.

He grinned up at her. 'Both. I'm not invited and I wouldn't want to go if I was.'

Surely Jonas didn't leave this engaging child alone while he was wining and dining Miss Eager Lips? She had to know. 'And who looks after you while they're gone?'

'Septimus.'

Gemma eyed him in some surprise. 'Sounds like a spider.'

'Sep is our au pair. He's a student at catering college

who goes to classes during the day and makes our evening meal at night.'

Her surprise wasn't diminishing. 'Does he live with you?'

'Yes,' Daniel told her enthusiastically. 'He's great. When I'm on school holidays so is he. We have a smashing time.'

'Does Cheryl live with you, too?' she probed.

He shook his head decisively. 'No.'

'I see. And does she go with you and…er…Sep…on your outings?'

'No,' he said again. 'She only wants to come when Dad's there.'

I'll bet, Gemma thought glumly.

Jonas had a very nicely organised domestic set-up. No wonder he wasn't ready to rush into a committed relationship. He had Daniel, a capable, young, male au pair and an equally young blonde bimbo panting on the doorstep.

Where did he take the seductive Cheryl on those occasions when Daniel wasn't included? Not to McDonald's, that was for sure. This kind of place was where nondescript junior doctors fitted in best, and if that was the case, was she bothered?

Yes…and…no.

Yes, because she was envious of the attractive girl that she'd seen only once but wasn't likely to forget, and no, because she was getting to know Daniel and seeing Jonas at his most relaxed, which was still a far cry from how he'd been during the long weary months he'd spent saving her face.

'A penny for them?' he asked smilingly as they seated themselves.

'They're worth more than that,' she said solemnly.

He looked at her questioningly. 'Really?'

'Mmm,' she murmured with a chip poised in mid air.

'And are you going to tell us what they are?'

Daniel's big brown orbs were fixed on her over the top of a cheeseburger.

'No, not at the moment, but that doesn't say I won't some time.'

There was something in Jonas's thoughtful glance that she couldn't fathom. She didn't think for a moment that he was really interested in what was in her mind after the short, revealing conversation with his son, but he was watching her with an intensity that made her cheeks warm.

However, if they were tuning in to each other's vibes, Daniel wasn't. 'Where are we going afterwards, Dad?' he wanted to know. 'To the bowling alley?'

It seemed as if it was an effort for Jonas to take his attention off her, though she didn't know why. He turned his head slowly to look at the boy and then said absently, 'Nowhere, Daniel. It's mid-week. You're at school in the morning, and Gemma and I have a busy day ahead of us, too.'

Gemma got to her feet. He was right and, added to her work on the plastic surgery unit, she would be keeping an eye on her father. Had Roger been to see him? she wondered as she offered up a prayer of thanks for being given the chance to avoid him.

Having got the message that she was ready to be off, the man and the boy also stood up, and Gemma thought illogically that they all three had dark hair and eyes. Not a blond root amongst them, but the girl whom Daniel seemed wary of had her share—and so did Michaela.

The title of an old film came to mind—*Gentlemen Prefer Blondes*. She hoped that if that was the case with Jonas's father, it didn't apply to his son.

The ring of a mobile phone stored away in the pocket of Jonas's smart leather jacket brought forth a sigh from him, and Gemma thought immediately that there must be an emergency at the hospital.

She was wrong. As Jonas replied to the voice at the other end in flat monosyllables, Daniel whispered, 'It will be Cheryl. She's always ringing Dad on his mobile.'

When he'd finished speaking and was replacing the phone in his pocket, Jonas said, 'That was Cheryl. She's been dining out in the West End and discovered that she's left her purse at home. As the waiter is hovering with the bill she's calling for help.'

He saw that his son and the very fanciable member of his staff were wearing wide smiles and asked curiously, 'So what's the joke?'

'I'd just told Gemma who it would be,' Daniel said. 'Why doesn't Cheryl get a life?'

Hear!! Hear! Gemma applauded silently, her amusement increasing at the boy's unchildlike comment.

It seemed that his father saw no cause for humour. 'That's enough of that, Daniel,' he said sternly. 'What goes on between Cheryl and myself is our business. We are going to have to make a detour to settle her restaurant bill once we've dropped Gemma off, and I'd like to know where you picked up the expression that you've just come out with.'

'It's what Septimus says about her,' the boy said without guile.

'I see.'

Jonas's face had blanked, the sternness leaving it, and Gemma, her mirth draining away fast, thought glumly that if Jonas jumped to Cheryl's bidding like this there had to be some sort of understanding between them.

From the sound of it the relationship wasn't popular with Daniel and the au pair, who at that moment was a shadowy figure in the background. It wasn't what *she* wanted either, but Jonas's life was his own, and as he led the way to the car she wished that she could say the same about hers.

She hadn't liked the girl on the night they'd met and her

standing was even lower now. They'd been having a pleasant relaxing evening, just the three of them, but Cheryl had broken into it and now she, Gemma, was being bundled off home so that Jonas could sort out his stepmother's sister's predicament.

'Can't I stay at Gemma's while you go to see Cheryl?' Daniel asked, and as Gemma brought her thoughts into line she found Jonas eyeing her questioningly.

'That might be best, if you don't mind,' he said.

Mind! She didn't mind at all, except that it must be long past Daniel's bedtime and she felt bound to mention the fact.

'Yes, I know,' Jonas agreed briefly, 'but we're talking about half an hour, that's all.'

He smiled at his son, his good humour restored. 'You'll just have to give your neck and ears a miss tonight.' As the boy nodded in enthusiastic agreement he turned to Gemma. 'Let's go, then, or they'll have Cheryl in the kitchens, doing the washing-up, and she's not used to soiling her hands.'

Gemma swallowed back a selection of choice retorts and nodded mutely. What was the matter with him? she thought grimly. He, of all people, who never wasted a second of his working life, involved with a useless silver-spoon-in-the-mouth type of girl.

Maybe that was the answer. Jonas worked so hard, saving faces and various other parts of the anatomy, that he needed his personal life to be empty and frivolous to counteract the strain.

Or perhaps after his brief, disastrous marriage he wasn't in the market for deep relationships. If that was the case she might as well forget him.

When he pulled up in front of Gemma's house with a swish of tyres, she and Daniel got out quickly. As the boy looked around him curiously, Jonas rolled down the car window and said in a low voice, 'Why so solemn all of a sudden? I hope that you don't feel you're being lumbered with Danny. I promise I won't be long.'

Gemma dredged up a smile. 'I don't feel anything of the kind. It will be a pleasure to have him. I'll give him some supper while he's waiting. He's a lovely boy, Jonas, and deserves to be happy.'

'And you think he isn't?'

'Let's just say that he is...now, but if his life should change drastically who knows how he'll feel.'

'What are you trying to tell me?' he asked irritably. 'That the two of us should stay as we are for evermore?'

'Yes,' she snapped back. 'If that's best for Daniel.'

'Well, you certainly don't beat about the bush. Message received. Here am I thinking that for once my life is on the right track, only to find that you want to push me back into the sidings.'

The car was moving off and the last sentence came over his shoulder, echoing through the window into the night air. Gemma turned away and, putting her arm around the boy's shoulders, led him along the path towards the darkened porch, thinking as she did so that she had some nerve telling Jonas how to run his life when he'd never shown any interest in hers.

Yet why should he? It would seem that he had other things on his mind that were more pressing than anything that the likes of her might be involved in.

When she produced a glass of milk and biscuits for her small visitor Gemma watched with amusement as he polished them off. No one observing him would have credited that it was only half an hour since he'd last eaten. Noting her smile, Daniel asked curiously, 'Why are you laughing, Gemma?'

She gave him a quick hug. 'I'm just wondering if you've got hollow legs.'

'You mean because I'm hungry all the time?'

'Mmm.'

His mind already moving on, Jonas's son was looking around him. 'Do you live here by yourself?' he asked.

'No, I live with my father but, if you remember, he's in hospital. You saw him yesterday.'

He nodded. 'Yes. I do remember.' Then, bringing her attention sharply to bear, he asked, 'Haven't you got a mother?'

'Er…no,' Gemma told him carefully. 'She died some time ago.'

'Neither have I.' Daniel said, as if glad that they had a common footing. 'Dad keeps saying he'll do something about it when Grandad gets on to him, but I don't think he will because I once heard him say that he'd been bitten by her.'

There was a wobble in his voice now, whether from confusion, dismay, or just plain deprivation, she didn't know, but Gemma made haste to reassure him.

'It's a saying that people sometimes use when a person has let them down,' she explained gently. 'Once bitten, twice shy.'

'What does it mean?'

How did we get into this? she wondered grimly as he waited for an answer.

'It simply means that when a person has done something to hurt us, we aren't always ready to let it happen again. It doesn't mean that we've actually been bitten by them.'

'Oh, I see,' he said, munching on the last biscuit. Then he added, with the fast-switching mind of the child, 'Could we have the football results on, Gemma? I want to see how Tottenham Hotspur have got on. They had a football game tonight.'

'Yes, of course,' she agreed immediately, relieved that his brief reference to his absent mother had been just that—

a thought-provoking moment triggered by her own motherless state.

'Yippee! They've won!' he cried, and at that moment the doorbell rang.

'Hi, there,' Jonas said as he brought a rush of cold night air in with him. 'Everything all right?'

'Yes,' she told him, aware that he would find that hard to believe were she to tell him that his son had been discussing his lack of a mother. 'Tottenham won.'

His face had been sombre when she'd opened the door to him, but now he was smiling. 'Ah! Good! That will make Daniel happy. I would have taken him to watch the match but, as you know, I didn't get away from the hospital early enough and Sep had an evening lecture so he wasn't able to take him.'

Unable to contain her curiosity any longer Gemma asked, 'Did you find Cheryl?'

'Yes. She's in the car. I'm taking her home after I've seen Daniel safely between the sheets. Septimus should be back by now so he'll keep an eye on him.'

'Where does she live?'

If she sounded nosy she couldn't help it. The urge to find out all she could about the blonde was overwhelming.

'Cheryl shares an apartment in St John's Wood with a couple of her yuppie friends,' he explained with a slightly surprised expression.

Driven on, she probed, 'And what does she do for a living?'

The surprised expression was deepening, the reply more brief. 'Beauty therapist.'

'That figures,' she remarked flatly.

'Huh?' Jonas questioned.

'Nothing. I was merely thinking out loud.'

'Right,' he said with continuing brevity. 'We'll be

off…and thanks, Gemma, for having Dan. He's short of some sensible female company.'

Her mouth twisted. She was aching for this man, longing to be part of his life…and she'd just been labelled 'sensible female company'.

It wouldn't have mattered so much if he hadn't left them to go dashing off to rescue the exquisite, golden-haired Cheryl, but the fact remained that he had and from where *she* was standing the girl appeared to be second on his list of priorities after Daniel.

Jonas had seen her expression and, putting his finger under her chin, he raised her face to his and kissed her lightly on the mouth.

By a supreme effort of will she didn't give in to the magic of his touch. Didn't let the brief caress throw her into a quivering heap.

Instead she acknowledged the salute with a gracious inclination of her head and then turned away to take Daniel's jacket down from the coat stand in the hall.

He was still absorbed in the sports results and Jonas had to call him twice before he appeared, still beaming from the news of his team's win.

Perversely Gemma walked out with them to the car. It would have been simpler to have bade them goodbye at the door but the desire for another glimpse of the girl who had spoilt her evening was too strong to ignore.

The glamour was still there, but as Cheryl wound down the car window the light from the streetlamp made her hair look brassy and her skin less creamy than before.

'We've met before, haven't we?' she drawled. 'That night at Jonas's apartment. I presume that you're one of his young hopefuls.'

'Really?' Gemma said coolly, comparing the pert face in front of her with a mental vision of Sally Graham's battered features. 'You should call in to see us on the plastic surgery unit some time. Junior doctors like myself can't afford to pose as "hopefuls". We've got to be sure about everything we do. The "hopefuls" are the patients, the ones who are praying that we'll be able to put them back together again.'

Jonas was round the other side of the car, tucking Daniel in, and had missed the conversation, but now he was back by her side, observing her grim expression and the red, smiling mouth of his other passenger.

He made no comment. With a brief salute he got behind the wheel and drove off.

If the evening had been a mixture of pain and pleasure, the following morning proved to be even more turbulent, though for different reasons.

After a restless night during which Jonas and the blonde Cheryl had figured largely in her dreams, Gemma arrived at the hospital to find her father with a temperature.

The sister on Men's Surgical informed her that he had started to feel ill during the night and that the orthopaedic consultant, on arriving, had decided that he had an infection in the area that had been operated on and had to be given antibiotics.

Gemma frowned. Her dad had been fine when she'd left him the previous night and as she'd heard nothing from Roger he must have been all right when he had visited him in the late evening.

Obviously, as the sister had explained, his condition had become less stable during the night. Infection after an operation was not uncommon and no doubt the medication the orthopaedic surgeon had recommended would clear it up, but Harry looked hot and fretful, with the novelty of his hospital stay wearing thin.

After a few gentle words of comfort and the promise that she would be back to check on him shortly, she put in an appearance on the unit.

She was ten minutes late and Peter said sarcastically, 'What's this, then? The alarm not go off?'

Gemma sighed. 'My dad is poorly this morning. I've been checking up on him.'

'Oh. I see.'

James was hovering. 'Sally Graham's parents are waiting to see Jonas. There appears to be a touch of hysteria present.'

Gemma eyed him anxiously. 'Not with Sally!'

'No, the parents.'

'Why, what's wrong?'

'They were away on holiday when she got hurt and have only just got here. When they saw that her jaws were wired they weren't happy. I don't think they're aware of what's entailed and the kid is breaking her heart because what bit of confidence Jonas and you have given her is fast ebbing away while they're ranting on.'

'The fools!' Gemma hissed under her breath. 'Where is Jonas? Hasn't he arrived?'

A vision of the long, lean, length of him between satin sheets with a pair of inviting red lips and various other parts of the anatomy on offer came to mind and she felt sick, but it was only momentary as his voice said briskly from behind, 'And what's this? A staff meeting? Am I to take it that the patients don't need us this morning?'

Gemma was already on edge and the implied rebuke pushed her over it. 'No, you are not!' she said with a chill to her voice. 'We were discussing Sally Graham's distress...and that of her parents, who don't seem too pleased about her treatment.'

'I see. Well, in that case you and I had better have a word with them, Dr Bartlett. It might make them feel better when they've seen the role model.'

As they marched to a small side ward where the injured girl had been placed, Jonas said, 'Last night you were sweet reason itself, but this morning you're decidedly tetchy. Why?'

'I didn't sleep very well,' she said stiffly, 'and Dad is quite poorly this morning. He's got an infection.'

'Drat!' he said quickly. 'You could both do without that.'

'There are a few things I could do without,' she said with the chill still in her voice.

He stopped in mid-stride and pulled her round to face him. 'What do you mean? Daniel and I latching onto you? Because if you do…you have only to say the word.'

Sudden tears stung her eyes and for some ridiculous reason Gemma wanted to turn back the clock to when she'd been in the same situation as Sally Graham and Jonas had been her laughing saviour.

She might have been in great pain and distress but her feelings then had been so simple and uncomplicated…until she'd heard he was contemplating matrimony and that very thing had resulted in their present situation. *She* was pining for his attention and *he* had been bitten but wasn't averse to some dalliance with a willing partner.

'But talking about that son of mine,' he was continuing, 'you've made a hit there. Dan has been telling Sep about you and the young rip is bursting to make your acquaintance.'

Still peeved, she said coldly, 'How old is he?'

'Nineteen.'

'Huh! I'm not into cradle-snatching.'

'I'm glad to hear it,' he answered coolly.

With his hand on the doorhandle of the private ward Jonas paused. 'Time to put personal matters on hold, Dr Bartlett.'

He reached out and tucked a stray tendril of glossy brown hair behind her ear. 'We have to get on with saving faces and reassuring anxious parents.'

The parents in question were seated on either side of

their daughter's bed, and when he saw the two doctors
Sally's father, a big burly man in a smart business suit, go
quickly to his feet.

'Does my girl have to have this contraption in her
mouth?' he rasped. 'She could choke!'

Jonas eyed him with calm compassion. 'Yes, I'm afraid
she does, Mr Graham. As you can see, your daughter's face
has been seriously injured and, after manipulating the fractures into place, I had no choice but to wire her jaw because
of orthodontic problems. The treatment might seem severe,
but in the long run it will be worth it.'

His wife had been listening anxiously. 'What is she going to look like at the end of it, Doctor?' she shrilled.
'That's what I want to know.'

Gemma eyed her soberly. If Sally's battered features had
been able to show any expression she felt that there would
be utter despair there. This discussion should be in private,
without the injured girl listening in mute distress.

It seemed as if Jonas was of the same opinion. 'Why
don't we leave Sally to get some rest and continue our chat
in my office?' he suggested equably.

The father was having none of it. 'No way! She's entitled
to know what's going on.'

'Sally does know,' Jonas informed him. 'Dr Bartlett and
I talked to her yesterday and were able to reassure her.'

'Reassure! She'll be disfigured for life after this lot.'

Gemma stepped forward. 'Not necessarily,' she told him,
thinking that it was time she said her piece. 'I had a similar
accident. In fact, my injuries were almost identical to
Sally's. I had to have my jaw wired, too, but Dr Parry saved
my face.' She smiled. 'As you can see.'

When she'd finished speaking there was silence as the
fraught couple took in what had been said. Sally's father
slumped back down on to the chair that he'd sprung up
from at their entrance and her mother burst into tears of

relief, while the girl eyed her gratefully from beneath swollen eyelids.

'Well done,' Jonas said softly as they left the stricken family. 'It isn't often that a plastic surgeon has an example of his skills to call upon whenever the need arises.'

'My pleasure,' she breathed. 'You gave me back my life when you resurrected my face.'

'So do you feel that you owe me something?' he asked with a quirky smile.

'Yes, of course. I always will.'

'Then marry me, Gemma. It would be the sensible thing to do.'

They'd been walking down the main corridor of the hospital, two dark-haired, white-coated members of staff, but now Gemma was riveted to the spot, her eyes wide with amazement, her face bleached with shock.

'What did you say?' she gasped.

'I think you heard me the first time.'

'Sensible!' she croaked. 'Being proposed to is one of the most romantic moments in a woman's life, but you can only see a marriage between us as a "sensible" undertaking!'

She didn't give him the chance to reply—she was too upset—and with her voice thickening she went on, 'I don't see myself as a suitable wife for a man who has got something going with someone else. Although that fact rather puts the unsuitability on your shoulders.'

A porter eyed them curiously as he trundled a skip of soiled bedclothes to the laundry room, and Gemma's lip curled. 'And while we're on the subject of suitability, what a delightful setting for a proposal. Not a secluded table in a nice restaurant, a gondola on a moonlit canal in Venice or a golden beach.

'Oh, no! A hospital corridor, perfumed not with the aroma of good food, or with the sound of lapping water— unless the slosh of a cleaner doing a mopping-up operation comes into that category—but with the smell of disinfectan and the distant squeak of the wheels of the library trolley Who could ask for more?'

He was laughing! Actually laughing! 'So it's yes?'

'Don't be ridiculous!' she hissed. 'If it were a meal you were offering I'd be obliged to tell you that you'd missed out the main ingredient.'

His mirth had gone as quickly as it came. 'And you think that a marriage can't work without it? That sexual chem istry, trust and respect aren't enough?'

'No! I don't think those things are enough.' she said icily. 'Ask me again when you can get your tongue around the one word that every woman needs to hear—that is, if the pushy Cheryl hasn't got it tied in a knot!'

'You've got it all wrong,' he told her flatly. 'Think about it and when you've calmed down give me your answer.'

If she'd heard his request Gemma gave no sign. She was walking away from him with a speed that showed how desperate she was to get away from the intolerable situation he had created.

CHAPTER SIX

BACK in his consulting room Jonas sat gazing into space, his fingers drumming absently on the desk top. There was a wry smile on his face. Gemma Bartlett had just put him in his place in no uncertain terms and he supposed he'd asked for it.

It was only the previous night that she'd made it clear that she wasn't in the market for happy families and now—this morning—what had he done? Made a complete fool of himself for reasons that he wasn't quite sure about.

Had it been because Cheryl was getting out of hand, making it clearer with every day what she wanted of him...and he wasn't clear in his mind about what his response should be? Or because Daniel had said on the way to school, 'Dad, if you ever find me a new mother, I'd like it to be Gemma.'

'You haven't known her five minutes!' he'd said in amazed disbelief, 'and how do you know she'd agree?'

'She might...if you persuaded her. You can always make Cheryl do what you want...so why not Gemma?'

He'd had to laugh at the boy's logic. The things he made Cheryl do had no similarity to anything he might require of his most able member of staff.

He continued to sit there in brief respite with the great throbbing heart of the hospital around him, reasoning with himself that there could be another motive for what he'd done.

She was a Cinderella, in spite of having a loving father and an ardent suitor breathing down her neck. There was a solitary air about her that worried him and, after all, he did have a sort of responsibility towards her. She had been a patient of his, once.

He could have gone on all day, inventing reasons for his insane, ridiculously phrased marriage proposal, but there was a clinic of outpatients waiting for him—people with a lot more on their minds than trying to justify having behaved like an idiot.

The parents of a six-week-old baby were the first to present themselves when Jonas went downstairs to face those who needed his skills, and both he and James, who was assisting him this time, were immediately aware that here was another distressed couple.

It had obviously been a great shock to them when the baby was born with a cleft palate, and they were anxious to know how soon the problem could be dealt with and whether any other children they might have would be similarly affected.

Before he was ready to answer their questions Jonas had some of his own. 'How are you coping with baby's feeding?' That was the first.

The young mother managed a smile. 'I haven't been able to breast-feed Petra, but she manages to take my milk when I've expressed it into a bottle with a large hole in the teat.'

He nodded approvingly. 'That's good...that your daughter is managing to get the nourishment she needs without too much trouble. Far better than her having to be spoon-fed or fed by some other laborious method.'

'Has there ever been a case of a cleft palate before in either of your families?' That was his next question. 'It can be hereditary and comes from a breakdown in normal fusion during the early stages of pregnancy.'

They both shook their heads emphatically and the husband said raggedly, 'No way. We wouldn't be likely to forget something like that! We want to know how soon you can do something about it, Doctor!'

'I normally operate on a cleft *lip* when a child is three months old,' he told them, 'as against when it is newborn. By that time the baby has added to its birth weight and is in a stronger state to undergo the surgery. It isn't exactly a dangerous operation but it needs careful nursing afterwards with an alternative airway and feeding arrangements. So I shall send for your little one in six weeks' time to repair the lip and will operate on the palate when she's twelve months old.'

'What's involved when you do her lip?' the anxious young father asked.

'It will be a case of incising the centre of the upper lip as it is now and bringing it downwards to where a normal lip would be. As that will leave a space, I will then move tissue across from the side to fill the gap.

'Baby's nostril will have to be brought into line to give it the right shape, and once all that has been achieved the new lip will be held in place with a metal hoop taped across it or, alternatively, with Steristrips. They will stay in position for four to five days and once they've been removed you'll be able to take your daughter home, knowing that she's halfway to looking normal.'

When the small family had left Jonas said to James, 'I have no doubt that to them their baby is beautiful, but the trick that nature has played on her face is a cruel one. She's in the same category as Sally Graham—here to have her face saved—but for vastly different reasons.'

With his mind on a certain young doctor who was decidedly cheesed off with him at that moment—and not without cause—he thought that there was nothing more gratifying in his job than to give a beautiful woman back her face...or a young baby the chance to be like all the rest.

In plastic surgery he saw it all, the disfiguring horror of burns, accidents and congenital defects, amongst other things, and if he wasn't the bouncy medic Gemma remembered from long ago, he was no less dedicated.

Giving in to a sudden urge to see her again—to gauge just how mad she really was at his crazy proposal—he went to seek her out the moment his clinic was over, only to find that she'd taken an early lunch and had gone to Men's Surgical to see her father.

As the morning had progressed it had taken all Gemma's powers of concentration to keep her mind on the needs of the patients in the unit.

In a less demanding job she mightn't have managed it, but in health care 'need' was the key word, whether in medicine-related treatment, actual surgery, the reassurance that the sick were always desperate for...or the counselling required when no earthly remedies were available and the sufferer was about to embark upon that last frightening journey into the unknown.

Fortunately in plastic surgery the last situation was rarely present as almost all cases admitted to the unit were of a remedial nature, but there was still plenty of fear and trauma as the ailing population came asking to be made whole again.

Listening patiently to the uneasy questions of a fifty-year-old woman who was waiting to go down to Theatre to have tendons repaired and the swan's-neck shape of the fingers corrected on a hand that was distorted with rheumatoid arthritis, Gemma was able to give the nervous patient her full attention. Likewise the elderly man who was going to need a full-thickness skin graft after the removal of a rodent ulcer.

But the moment she left the ward and made her way to where she'd left her father feeling anything but well a couple of hours earlier, the words that she'd pushed to the back of her mind all morning took over like a mocking chant inside her head.

'Marry me, Gemma! Marry me, Gemma! Marry me...'

Had he really said that? Had Jonas really asked her to marry him?

Of course he had. She wasn't going crazy and the reason he'd given had made it feel like being doused with a bucket of cold water. If he'd told her he loved her, adored her, couldn't live without her, she would have melted at the thought, but it hadn't been like that.

Maybe he was of the opinion that she was just the type to fit in when it came to the basics and—as a pair of pouting red lips came to mind—that someone else would be around for the more exciting moments.

If she'd felt that her Dad and Roger were manipulative, this was in a different dimension. It made *their* machinations seem like child's play.

At this point in her confused reasoning she arrived beside her father's bed and her own affairs had to be put to one side as she observed him anxiously.

'I'm feeling a little better,' he told her, 'but I'm still feeling hot and fuzzy in the head.'

'He will improve as the antibiotics take effect,' a hovering nurse said. Gemma nodded. No need to tell her that. She was fully aware of the situation, but when the patient was one's own flesh and blood the anxiety was just as great as anyone else's.

'Go and get some lunch, Gemma,' Harry suggested. 'There's nothing you can do here and your break will be gone before you've had anything to eat.'

'I'm not hungry,' she said flatly. She wasn't. She'd been offered a tempting dish earlier, which she would have been delighted to partake of if the main ingredient hadn't been missing, and now she had no appetite at all.

However, the fact remained that Jonas was expecting an

answer to his cold proposal and before the day was out she would have to face him again.

What was she going to say? There was only one answer…and it wasn't yes.

After forcing down coffee and a sandwich, she presented herself on the unit once more and saw to her relief that Jonas wasn't present. Any respite was welcome. At the moment she felt as if she didn't care if she never saw him again.

He didn't show up until her stint was almost up, and when she heard him tell Peter that he'd been called away to attend a private patient and would be going out again within the next few minutes Gemma hid herself away in the ward kitchen until he'd gone.

'So Jonas does have private patients after all,' James said as they discarded their white coats, he anxious to get home to his wife and family, and she about to spend some time with her father, before going home to the empty house.

'I suppose it's only to be expected,' he went on. 'In this area there must be plenty of women who have the time and the money to spend on improving their appearance.' He smiled. 'My wife would be beautiful to me no matter how she looked.'

'Lucky Mrs Brice to be so cherished,' Gemma said wistfully.

James laughed. 'And lucky me to have her as my wife.'

'Indeed,' she agreed, and turned away before he saw the yearning on her face.

The last thing she wanted to hear about, today of all days, was a happy marriage. Churlish though the thought might be, she couldn't help it.

It was eight o'clock when she got home, after chatting with her father and making small talk with Roger who had called in after evening surgery. Harry was gradually improving and when Gemma had left the two men engrossed in surgery talk she had been much easier in her mind than she'd been that morning.

Roger had made no attempt to either detain her or accompany her when she left, for which she had been thankful, but she'd been aware of his scrutiny whenever he'd thought she hadn't been looking, and she'd thought that he would have had even more reason to stare if he'd known that earlier in the day Jonas Parry had proposed to her.

As the front door swung inwards the house felt cold and cheerless and Gemma thought that it matched her mood exactly. She'd been relieved not to have seen Jonas during the afternoon, but now she was wishing that she had. There was no way she'd be able to sleep with the thought of him waiting for her answer. She should have sought him out, instead of prolonging the agony.

On a sudden impulse she turned and went back outside. If the traffic was reasonable she could be at his place in twenty minutes, and once the deed was done she could go home with an easy mind.

Easy mind! What was that? Before Jonas had come back into her life she'd been overworked, energetic and career-minded but with her own brand of tranquillity. The rest of it still applied but her calmness of spirit had been diminishing and what had happened between the two of them today had wiped out what had been left.

As she rang the doorbell of the Pimlico apartment Gemma was having second thoughts. She should have stayed put...let him make the first move. It was cheapening herself to come chasing round to his place to tell him that he could get lost! That she had no intention of marrying him, and that—

Any further self-castigation was halted when the door opened and a gangling youth with blond hair scraped back in a ponytail stood eyeing her with distinct approval.

'Yes?' he questioned.

This young male, enveloped in a white apron, had to be
Septimus, the au pair, she decided, friend of Daniel and of
the opinion that Cheryl should get a life—a fact that would
have made her warm to him even if he'd had two heads
and been covered in animal hair.

'Er…I'm Gemma Bartlett,' she told him as her sense of
purpose drained away. 'I work with Jonas. Is he in?'

He shook his head. 'Gone to the airport to pick up his
old man,' he said laconically. 'Michaela couldn't go as she
has a performance tonight.'

'I see. I'll catch him another time, then.'

As she turned to go Daniel's voice came from behind
him. 'Gemma! Don't go. Dad will be back any minute.'

He looked scrubbed and clean in black pyjamas with a
luminous Bart Simpson on the front and a lump came up
in her throat.

She was about to pass up the chance of sharing in his
life and why? Out of pique…because she wanted more than
Jonas was prepared to give?

Scraping up a smile, she said, 'It looks as if your neck
and ears haven't escaped tonight.'

He grinned. 'Hmm. Dad said he was going to inspect
them when he came back.' There was still a question in his
eyes. 'Are you going to come inside? I could show you my
Playstation.'

The laconic Sep was moving back to allow her over the
threshold, as if supporting the boy's invitation, and instead
of listening to common sense Gemma went inside.

Within seconds she was in Daniel's bedroom, being
shown the electronic wizardry of the Playstation, her young
host perched raptly on the edge of the chair while the fair-
haired au pair leaned against the doorpost in his big white
apron.

He sighed above the bleeping of the Playstation. 'I must
go back to my kitchen, Gemma. I have work to do. There

is a feast to be prepared for the return of the prodigal father.'

'Don't take any notice of Sep,' Daniel said over his shoulder. 'He's only got the potatoes to peel. Dad's picking up a take-away on his way home from the airport.'

'And what about ze afters?' Sep said with an atrocious foreign accent. 'It ees ze big job taking ze ice cream out of ze freezer and there ees the young master's supper to prepare as he ees due to go to hees bed in ze next ten minutes.'

'Dad said I could wait up to see Grandad,' Daniel reminded him.

'Yes, he did,' Septimus agreed, 'and if I'm not mistaken, that's the front door now.'

Gemma froze. This wasn't how she'd planned it, for Jonas to find her ensconced in his home on his return from meeting his father. She'd anticipated finding him alone, having a quick decisive word with him and making an even speedier exit.

She was on her feet in a flash. If there was a back door she was going to use it. It was too late. She heard footsteps on the stairs and almost simultaneously the man she'd come to see was looking at her in some amazement over Sep's shoulder.

'Gemma!' he breathed. 'What a surprise.'

She didn't speak but her expression told him that surprise though it might be, it wasn't in the same category as the one he'd sprung on her on the hospital corridor that morning.

If he was getting the message he didn't show it. Instead he said calmly, 'I've been to pick my father up at the airport. He's downstairs.' He held out his hand. 'Come, I'll introduce you.'

This was going from bad to worse, she thought, ignoring the outstretched hand. The more she became involved with his family the harder it would be to break the spell Jonas held over her. But she could hardly refuse to meet the man who had cast his own kind of spell on the beautiful Michaela Martin and, that being so, she inclined her head in gracious agreement and preceded him down the stairs.

Before they reached the hallway below Jonas reached out from behind and brought her to a halt. 'Why are you here, Gemma?' he asked quietly. 'Because of this morning?'

She was a step below him, looking up into the face that haunted her with its strong lines and the brown eyes that had seemed softer of late.

'Yes,' she replied with assumed calm, as if refusing a second marriage proposal in a week was run of the mill. As she braced herself to say what had to be said he butted in first.

'Forget what I said. I acted totally out of character. A remark of Daniel's on the way to school sent my thoughts off at a tangent and I spoke entirely on impulse.'

So he was already regretting it, she thought as a tight little pain encircled her heart. She should be relieved about that surely, not feeling as if the ground had just shot from under her feet. After all, hadn't she been about to tell him that the only emotion she'd felt at his proposal had been one of anger at the love-lacking nature of it?

'That's fine, then,' she said, trying to keep her voice steady. 'We're both of the same opinion.'

'Meaning?'

'That you forgot for a moment that we're poles apart. You are my boss. You live in this elegant apartment that makes the house that my mum and dad shared look extremely basic, and you have two beautiful women in your life in Michaela Martin and her sister. With regard to your emotions, it's plain to see who makes *your* heart beat faster…and it isn't me. Why insult me with a spur-of-the-moment proposal of marriage that you didn't mean?'

She was praying that his father wasn't somewhere tuning into this conversation but at that moment she couldn't have stopped the flood of words if she'd wanted to.

'I had no intentions of insulting you,' Jonas said evenly, 'but are you aware that even on such short acquaintance you have captured Daniel's heart? He said this morning that if I ever wished to present him with a new mother he would like it to be you.'

'So that was why you said what you did?' she said slowly, thinking that given the chance she could love the son as much as the father. But there was no way she could accept being mother to Daniel without being Jonas's cherished wife. 'You saw me fitting into the mother slot, did you, but that was all?'

Before he could reply she went on, 'I'm very fond of him, too, and maybe I could join them when he and Sep go out during the Christmas holidays. We could have some fun…without strings attached.'

'So you would prefer the company of a laid-back student to mine—or the pedantic GP's,' he remarked with a set look on his face.

'It would give you the opportunity to spend some time with the person that you really want to be with,' she parried back.

'And who might that be?'

'You've already treated me like a fool once today. Don't do it again,' she warned.

As Jonas opened his mouth to reply, a door at the end of the hallway opened and a craggy face beneath a shock of white hair jutted out.

'I've phoned Michaela and I'm going round to the theatre after we've eaten,' his father said. On seeing his son and a strange young woman poised at the foot of the stairs, he brought into view the body that went with the face.

'Dad, allow me to introduce Gemma Bartlett,' Jonas said

calmly, as if they'd just been discussing the weather. 'Gemma is on my team in the plastic surgery unit.'

As Gemma stepped forward to shake hands, keen grey eyes looked her over from a tanned face that had the same strong lines as his son's, and it wasn't hard to understand why an actress in her late thirties had been attracted to this fit-looking sixty-year-old.

'Nice to meet you, young lady,' Mr Parry senior said, and with a shrewd glance in his son's direction added, 'Are we likely to be seeing more of you?'

Gemma could feel her colour rising. 'Er…I don't think so, Mr Parry. I'd just called round with a message for Jonas and I'm about to leave.'

'I see. Well, you never know, we might meet again. And the name is Stuart, Dr Bartlett. Stuart Parry.' He put an affectionate arm around Jonas's shoulders. 'Father of this reclusive son of mine and grandad to young Daniel. You've perhaps observed that this household is one person short?' He bent and whispered conspiratorially, 'But I'm not supposed to comment on it.'

As her eyes took in the affectionate exasperation on Jonas's face, Gemma thought that the sooner she removed herself from this tinder-box situation the better.

Little did Stuart Parry know that his joking remark was on a subject that had been very recently discussed with no joy on either side.

'Grandad!' Daniel's voice cried from the top of the stairs, and the tension was broken as he came leaping down two at a time and flung himself into the older man's arms, while Septimus, who had been close on his heels, headed for the kitchen.

'Have you come by car?' Jonas asked as Gemma edged towards the front door. 'Or do you need a lift?'

She shook her head, suddenly unutterably weary. 'No. I don't need a lift. My car is on the road outside.' Her eyes went to the doting grandfather and the smiling boy. 'I think that your father is wrong, Jonas,' she said gravely. 'This household has everything it needs.' As a vision of those pouting red lips came to mind she continued, 'Don't spoil it for Daniel. Whatever he thinks of me, I would say that he's totally happy.'

With a farewell wave to the boy who would have liked her to be his mother she went—out into the cold night and home to the empty house once more, this time with more desolation in her than before.

Another day, another dawn. As Gemma lay back against the pillows, savouring the last few moments before greeting the chilly pre-Christmas morning, the events of the previous night came crowding back.

It was a good thing she hadn't gone to Jonas's apartment with the intention of accepting his proposal, she thought dismally as she snuggled under the covers. She would have died of mortification if she'd said yes, only to be informed that he hadn't meant it.

But, then, never in a thousand years would she have agreed to marry a man who was clearly attracted to someone else, even if he did have a delightful son. Jonas Parry had been her teenage idol and from there he had progressed to being the man she would adore for all time and nothing less than him loving her in return would do.

As she showered listlessly, reluctant to face the day, Gemma told herself, It's not long until Christmas. Concentrate on that, instead of wishing for the moon. Dad will be home by then. The two of you have managed to have a reasonable time during other festive seasons, so why not once again? At least Roger won't be breathing down your neck if he does the usual thing and visits his folks in the Isle of Man. All you have to do is keep your mind away from thoughts of Jonas partying with the glitzy Cheryl…and Daniel's face on Christmas morning.

Sally Graham's boyfriend was by her bedside when Gemma arrived on the ward at eight o'clock and she looked at him in surprise. It was very early for visiting. The hours were normally two until eight, seven days each week, but the fit-looking youngster with the economical haircut had a good reason for his presence.

'I'm in the navy and I've been away on manoeuvres, Doctor,' he said. 'I'm due back in a couple of hours. I only heard about what had happened to Sal last night.'

Angry blue eyes were observing the misshapen face of the girl in the bed. 'It was one of my mates who took her pillion-riding and he'll have me to deal with when I see him.'

Gemma eyed Sally sympathetically. It was bad enough to have injured her face so seriously, without her boyfriend finding out that she'd been in the company of someone else. Her manner was sheepish enough to indicate that she'd been involved with the other youth.

As Gemma checked the night staff's report on her progress he came to stand beside her and asked in a low voice, 'Will she always look like this…her face all scrunched up?'

She shook her head and gave him a reassuring smile. 'No. The swelling and bruising will go eventually and when the wires have been removed from her jaw she should begin to look more like herself.'

He nodded doubtfully and Gemma thought that once again she was going to have to bring back the past to assist the present.

'The same thing happened to me a few years ago and *I've* recovered,' she said gently.

He goggled at her, taking in the smooth skin where the marks of surgery were now almost invisible, the delicate jawline and the kind hazel eyes that told him it was the truth he was hearing.

'I don't believe it!' he breathed.

Her smile was back. 'You have to...and Sally is being treated by the same plastic surgeon who saved my face.'

The lad swallowed hard and Gemma thought that whatever Sally had been up to in his absence he was in love with her and hopefully she, Gemma, had helped him to absorb the shock of his girlfriend's injuries.

At the bottom of the ward fourteen-year-old Blake Thomas was seated at the table, doing a jigsaw with his one good hand. The other was secured across his chest, with his damaged fingers wired into position and then sewn into the soft pouch of flesh which had been created when Jonas had made an incision in his opposite armpit two weeks previously.

The boy had been rushed into Accident and Emergency with his frantic parents by his side, after fiddling with machinery on his father's farm. At the time of admission it had looked as if Blake would lose his fingers. His hand had been a mangled mess. The bones had been badly crushed and the skin ripped away with the force of the blades it had come into contact with. In the ambulance, paramedics had given the boy painkilling injections and had sprayed ice over the injured area.

When Jonas had seen the extent of his injuries he'd told Gemma and James, 'I'm going to try a new kind of treatment that plastic surgeons are using with some success.

'If it works, skin from the armpit will grow around the damaged fingers. Even the crushed bones might start to grow again, but we'll have to wait and see.' To the boy, who was more anxious that his hand should be saved to hold a cricket bat than a pen, he'd said comfortingly, 'A couple of weeks and we'll know the answer, young Blake.'

The lad had nodded miserably. He'd messed about with

something he'd been warned to keep clear of and was paying a harsh price.

Tuning into his dejection, Jonas had given him a comforting pat on the shoulder. 'We'll have to see if we can get one of the test cricketers to come in and cheer you up.'

That had perked him up. 'Really?'

'We can try, can't we, Dr Bartlett?' Jonas had said, and as their glances had held Gemma had thought that where the job was concerned Jonas hadn't changed a bit. The fount of caring expertise was still flowing strongly.

It was his private life that somehow lacked purpose and yesterday she'd had positive proof of it—a marriage proposal which had been taken back before she'd even had time to refuse it.

Blake looked up as she drew near. 'Today's the day, eh, Doctor?' he said excitedly.

Gemma smiled. His excitement was understandable. He must be weary of having his arm fastened across his chest and eager to know the result of the unique treatment.

'Yes,' she agreed. 'As soon as Mr Parry arrives he's going to cut the stitches that have been holding your fingers in place, and then we'll see what has been happening to them.'

He eyed her blankly. 'Yes. I know that, but I'm talking about the cricketers. It's today they're coming to see me.'

Gemma eyed him laughingly. Typical of the young, he saw only the immediate future. Long-term matters were put to one side in the excitement of the visit by some of the England test team which Jonas had arranged.

'Yes, I can see that it's first things first,' she said with continuing amusement.

As she stood in a pool of light from the wintry sun that was struggling through the ward windows, Gemma wasn't aware that Jonas was watching them from the doorway at the far end of the ward, noting how its rays turned the dark swathe of her hair into burnished bronze and threw into relief the fine-boned contours of the face that was smiling down on the boy.

His face was solemn. The happenings of the day before were still uppermost in his mind. He still couldn't believe he had been such a fool as to propose to someone who had made it quite clear that he and Daniel were better staying as they were…as far as she was concerned.

His hand went to the damp patch on his shirt collar where he'd sponged off Cheryl's lipstick the moment he'd arrived at the hospital.

His smile was wry. That one was just as amorous at eight o'clock in the morning as she was last thing at night, whereas the young doctor who was lighting up the ward on this cold winter's morning had been as frosty as the time of year when she'd taken her leave of him last night.

CHAPTER SEVEN

GEMMA felt her nerve ends tighten when she looked up and found Jonas watching them. He'd caught her in a relaxed moment and if it made him think that she'd got no hang-ups from yesterday she was thankful for it.

There was no way that she wanted her hurt on display, either here in the hospital or outside, and with that thought in mind she greeted him with bland pleasantness when he appeared at her side.

'Good morning, Mr Parry. I think that Blake is more excited at the prospect of the visit of the cricketing VIPs than having his arm released,' she informed him.

'If I were him I'd feel the same,' he agreed with a smile, 'but as today he's going to have the pleasure of both I suggest that we deal with the arm first, while he's waiting for the other big event.

'Where's James Brice?' he wanted to know. 'I want you both to be in on this.'

'It's his day off, I'm afraid.'

'Right. Then it's just the two of us for the moment of truth, as Peter French isn't around either and Sister and her staff are otherwise engaged at the moment with a couple of skin grafts that I've arranged to have admitted this morning.'

Gemma nodded, straight-faced. 'Just the two of us,' Jonas had said. He wasn't to know that the brief phrase had brought all her longings to the fore, making her impersonal persona disappear like the air from a pricked balloon.

That was how she wanted it to be—just the two of them

or, correction, the three of them. There was no way she couldn't include Daniel.

'You're not listening, Gemma,' Jonas's voice said, coming from far away.

'Yes, I am,' she protested. 'I'm totally tuned in to the occasion.'

He eyed her thoughtfully. 'Good. I'm glad to hear it.' As he bent over the boy, 'How is your father this morning?'

'Much improved' she replied briefly.

'That also is good.'

'Yes, it is,' she agreed, wishing that the conversation was less stilted, but that was the best thing, wasn't it? That they should maintain a businesslike manner that didn't allow for any further embarrassment?

As Jonas removed the stitches that had held Blake's fingers cushioned in his armpit for two long weeks, Gemma felt the trepidation that such moments always brought. Would the skin have grown over the crushed fingers...or would nature have been less obliging?

Their two dark heads together, the surgeon and the junior doctor bent over the boy, and Jonas gave a low hiss of pleasure.

'It's worked!' he said triumphantly. 'See how the skin has attached itself to the fingertips, Gemma? When I've separated the hand from beneath the armpit we'll have this young man taken to X-ray to see what's been happening to the bones. I know that there'll be some grafting to do, but there could also be some small degree of healing, too, if we're lucky.'

The boy had a pleased smile on his face as he looked down on his hand.

'Does it hurt?' Gemma asked him.

'A bit,' he confessed, 'and so does my arm when I try to straighten it.'

'That's understandable,' Jonas told him. 'You've had it

in one position for two weeks. I'll get the physiotherapist to give you some exercises and it will soon loosen up.'

The ward sister was hovering, her new charges now settled, and Jonas turned to face her, explaining as he did so that he wanted Blake's hand to be X-rayed, once it had been released.

The boy was looking at him anxiously, and he laughed. 'I take it that your expression is not due to concern about the X-rays but rather from the fear that you mightn't be here when your famous visitors arrive. Yes?'

Blake nodded vigorously.

'We'll leave the separation and X-rays until the cricketers have been, Sister,' he said, 'and I'll be back to see him when they've gone.

'I'm going to see Sally Graham next,' he said as they left the boy to his anticipation. 'Have you seen her this morning?'

'Yes. Her boyfriend was visiting. Apparently he's in the navy and it was the first chance he's had.'

'So who was the guy on the bike?' he asked with mild curiosity.

'Apparently young Sally had two strings to her bow, as my mother used to describe it. A fashionable exercise in some quarters, it seems.'

'Why do I feel that remark was directed at me?' he questioned with a grim smile.

'I'm sure I don't know,' she replied innocently, 'unless it hit a sore spot.'

'The only sore spots in my life healed long ago,' he said coolly. 'You have to believe that.'

A nurse changing the linen on one of the beds was eyeing them curiously as they passed, and Gemma lowered her voice as she asked, 'So why did you look as if your light had been snuffed out when you first came here?'

They were almost at Sally's bed and, drawing Gemma

to one side, Jonas opened a door that led onto the corridor and ushered her through it.

'I object to discussing my private life in front of my patients,' he said flatly. 'In answer to the question, I wasn't aware that I presented such a gloomy profile. So tell me— does it still apply, or have I mellowed?'

'Sometimes I think you have…'

'And sometimes you think I haven't?' he chipped in, his voice getting cooler by the minute.

'Whatever you are, or were, you will always have my highest regard,' she said unsteadily.

It would have been pure joy to have added, 'and my love and adoration', but her father had spilt the beans on that one when Jonas had first come to the unit. The embarrassment of it was still in its raw stage and, together with yesterday's episode, she wasn't asking for another piece of humble pie.

Maybe that was the reason he'd come out with his outrageous proposal…because he knew that she cared for him, and expected that his adoring slave would settle for anything.

'Your expression rather gives the lie to that,' he was saying as she tuned back into the moment.

Gemma shook her head. 'No. I meant it, Jonas, with all my heart.'

He took a step towards her and as his hand came out to touch her she moved back. They were exposed on the hospital corridor…again. If they made any kind of physical contact she would be lost. The mere thought of his skin touching hers would have had her drowning in a sea of longing.

'Don't!' she muttered. 'Don't touch me, Jonas. I'm not here for your amusement!'

He was opening the door that would take them back onto

the ward, his face blanked of all expression, but as they approached Sally's bed he had one last thing to say.

'This can't go on, Gemma. We need to talk.'

'Huh! I think we've said what has to be said,' she flung back at him.

'I'll be the judge of that,' he told her grimly. Then, meeting the anxious eyes of the injured girl, he smiled the special smile that helped those who were suffering to cope.

Insanely, Gemma was jealous. Jonas was the miracle-worker when it came to making good those who were damaged, but he wasn't into repairing shattered emotions.

Perhaps it was because someone had once played havoc with his, she thought as her bleeper went, relaying a message that she was required in Casualty.

If Jonas felt the need to talk he made little effort to do so during the following week. Gemma was aware of his eyes on her several times as she went about her duties, but any conversation they had was essentially work-oriented, and if he would have preferred it to be otherwise he gave no sign.

In the middle of what seemed like a desert of non-communication there was a phone call from another member of his family that helped to make it more bearable.

'Call for you, Dr Bartlett,' the switchboard operator said late one afternoon when her bleeper made its presence felt.

'Right, put them through,' she said, and was surprised to hear Daniel's voice on the line.

'Gemma,' he said with childish directness, 'I break up from school on Thursday and Sep and I are going Christmas shopping on the Friday. Would you like to come with us?'

'I'd love to,' she told him, 'but it depends whether I can get the time off. I might be able to get a free afternoon but I can't manage the whole day.'

'It's in the afternoon that we're going. Do try and come,'

he coaxed. 'Sep says he hopes you will. You could send a message with Dad if you're free and we'll pick you up in a taxi.'

'Leave it with me and I'll be in touch,' she promised, thinking as she did so that it wouldn't be through the suggested channels!

For one thing, with the state of indifference between them at the moment, Jonas might not like being used as a messenger boy, and for another he might take a dim view of the woman who didn't want to be Daniel's stepmother cementing her relationship with his son to a further degree.

Yet he would have to know if she went with them—and approve—or she couldn't do it. The simplest solution would be for her not to be able to get the time off.

But with the contrariness of life, for once there was no shortage of staff, and the following day she rang the Pimlico apartment to say that, subject to his father's agreement, she would go shopping with Daniel and Sep on the coming Friday.

It was a woman's voice that answered and when Gemma explained the reason for the call it became clear that it was the brassy-haired Cheryl on the other end of the line.

'That will be fine,' she said pertly. 'You're the Gemma person, aren't you? Jonas's young assistant?'

'Yes, that's right,' she agreed drily. She could give this confident young madam a few years but wasn't in the mood to discuss it.

If Jonas ever inflicted that one on Daniel as stepmother he would be insane, she thought dismally as she replaced the receiver...and she wasn't going to be part of the shopping trip on Cheryl's say-so.

There was nothing else for it. She would have to speak to him about it, and she admitted to herself that she was grateful to have a reason for a conversation that wasn't health-related.

He was in his office, scrutinising a patient's X-rays, when she found him. When he saw her standing there in response to his command to enter, Jonas eyed her coolly.

'I have something to discuss with you,' she said warily as the chilly reception washed off on her.

'Ah, so you *do* think we need to talk?'

'Only briefly,' she parried, relieved that the ice was broken. 'Daniel wants me to spend Friday afternoon with Sep and him. They're going Christmas shopping and I wanted to make sure that it's all right with you.'

He's not exactly bubbling over at the idea, she thought as he frowned and rubbed his hands together.

'What's the attraction?' he asked snappily.

Gemma stared at him. 'What was that supposed to mean?'

'Spending some time with Daniel, of course. What else?'

Surely he didn't think she was pining to see the laconic Sep!

'Yes, carry on, then,' he said indifferently. 'Anything that pleases my son pleases me…but, Gemma…'

'Yes?'

'Don't let him get too fond of you. I don't want it to turn into a pattern of events.'

'Meaning?'

'Another vulnerable young person wearing their heart on their sleeve.'

'How dare you?' she cried. 'Throwing back at me what my father told you!'

'That wasn't what I meant!' he cried as she stormed out of his office, but it was too late. As he went to the door her straight departing back was the only thing to be seen.

As he returned to his desk and slumped into the chair behind it, the way she had described him came to mind. She'd said he was like someone whose light had gone out.

He reached for the phone and dialled home. That was no

longer so. In spite of everything, he'd never felt so alight with living in his life, and if Gemma Bartlett didn't want to hear about it he knew someone who did.

Jonas was away at a conference in Manchester for the rest of the week, and as the days dragged by Gemma knew that she should have been grateful that he wasn't around to patronise her.

How could he have said what he did? she asked herself a thousand times. Was it because he enjoyed referring to her feelings for him? He was cruel if it was. Cruel and gloating, but those were characteristics that had never applied to her adored 'saver of faces'.

'What's wrong, Gemma, girl?' her father asked one afternoon when she popped in to see him. 'Is it because Jonas Parry's not around?'

'No, of course not,' she assured him. 'It's the thought of Christmas coming, with you in here and me back home and wondering how we're going to spend it.'

'I'll be out before then,' he said stoutly, 'and reasonably mobile. In fact, Roger has asked us to spend Christmas with him and his relatives in the Isle of Man again. What do you think?'

He was eyeing her hopefully but he was wasting his time. There was no way she wanted to spend Christmas with Roger Croft. If she couldn't be with Jonas she didn't want to be with anybody, apart from her father.

'Why don't you go without me?' she suggested, 'As long as you feel up to it. I would trust you in Roger's care. He would see that you don't overdo it and I know it's what you want.'

'We could fly there, I suppose,' he said thoughtfully. 'It would be smoother than going by boat, but I'm not leaving you alone at Christmas time. So either you come with us or I don't go.'

'No problem,' she said easily. 'Jonas has invited me to spend Christmas with him and his family...you, too, if you'd like to join them.'

His face cleared. 'Tell him thanks just the same but I'd rather go with Roger, and now that I know you won't be alone it will be with an easy mind.'

Gemma turned away. It had been true, what she'd said. The only thing she hadn't told her father was that she hadn't accepted Jonas's invitation and there was little likelihood of it being repeated. But if it gave her dad peace of mind regarding herself it was worth the slight fib by omission.

'This is all depending on you being fit enough, you know,' she reminded him, and went to discuss his progress with the surgeon who had operated on him.

'Should be no problem,' he assured her. 'As long as he's travelling with another doctor and doesn't start swinging from the Laxey wheel when he's had one or two. We'll be discharging him towards the end of next week.'

So that was that, Gemma thought as she went back to the ward. If all went according to plan her father's Christmas was sorted, and if she *had* to spend her Christmas leave alone it would still be better than having Roger breathing down her neck in the Isle of Man.

When she left the hospital at Friday lunchtime Jonas still hadn't returned from the conference, and by then she was suffering from withdrawal symptoms. A hunger for the sight of his muscular frame, his thick, dark hair, and the cool caring competence of him was gnawing at her. She wondered dismally how she would cope if he disappeared out of her life, if he were to go elsewhere to continue his career with the pushy young blonde by his side.

When Daniel and Sep called for her in the early afternoon she had cheered up a little. There was no need to spoil the shopping spree for them just because she was feeling low, she'd told herself, and once she had joined them in the black London cab her spirits rose.

'I haven't got a car,' the gangling au pair informed her, 'and Jonas insisted that you weren't to be involved in chauffeuring us through the traffic.'

'When is your dad due back, Daniel?' she asked casually, aware of Sep's eyes taking in her soft curves and her face framed in unruly chestnut tendrils.

'Tonight,' the boy said, *his* glance on the Christmas lights which were coming on as darkness drew in over the capital. 'That's why I wanted to go shopping today, Gemma. I want to get Dad's present while he's not around.'

'What are you going to buy him?' she asked as his dark eyes glowed at the thought.

He hesitated. 'I'm not sure. I've got a few ideas but don't know which one to choose.'

'How about Cheryl—gift-wrapped?' Sep suggested with a grin.

Daniel's face clouded. 'Don't joke about it, Sep. I keep hoping that she'll do as you suggest.'

'What? Get a life of her own?'

'Yes.'

'But maybe that isn't what Big Daddy wants,' the youth said with a shrug of his shoulders.

Gemma glared at him. Neither she nor Daniel wanted to hear about Jonas's relationship with his stepmother's sister. Taking the offensive, she said coolly, 'I can only think that having brought Cheryl's name into the conversation you have some interest in her yourself.'

As the bright colour flooded his face her eyes widened. She'd scored a hit. It would seem that the confident young blonde had two admirers in the one household, but Sep wouldn't stand a chance beside Jonas—not in stature, personality or looks—more was the pity!

The shops were extra bright and colourful, with a tempting array of seasonal goods, and as they strolled around them Gemma wished it was appropriate for her to make a gift to the man she ached to have in her arms.

There were a thousand things she would have liked to have given him and top of the list was herself. How would he feel if *she* was delivered to him gift-wrapped? Embarrassed? Put out? The waif and stray he must have been feeling sorry for when he'd called her Cinderella?

Daniel had chosen a silk tie with trumpets on it for his father, and had totally amazed her by vouching the information that his dad played that particular instrument.

'He's good, too, Gemma,' he'd informed her as Sep had nodded in agreement. 'Dad always says that it would be a lot less hassle being a busker than having to piece people together again.'

'Really!' she'd murmured, staggered at the thought of Jonas on a windswept pavement playing the 'Last Post'. She found herself laughing at the thought. Hardly that! Buskers played popular tunes.

They were in the men's department of London's most famous store, with Sep feigning faintness at the prices, when Daniel said, 'Look! There's Dad!'

As his two companions followed the direction of his delighted gaze they had to agree that he wasn't mistaken. Jonas was obviously back in town and, disastrously, he wasn't alone.

Cheryl was hanging onto his arm like a limpet and he wasn't objecting.

However, he wasn't so engrossed in his companion that he hadn't seen them, and at Daniel's welcoming cry he came over, gently disengaging the girl's grasp as he did so.

'So here you are,' he said buoyantly, hugging his son to him, but Gemma was aware that although he had Daniel in an affectionate embrace his eyes were on her.

Why, she didn't know, but he was observing her as if

she were an X-ray plate or suchlike, from which he had to make a diagnosis.

'And where are all the bags of Christmas shopping?' he asked in assumed surprise. 'Or haven't you started yet?'

Before they could reply Cheryl butted in, 'We've done ours, haven't we, Jonas?'

At the smugly presented comment he lifted dark brows in dubious surprise and replied, '*You* have, my dear. *I* shall do mine when I get a moment to myself.'

'Yes. That goes for me, too,' Gemma agreed with smooth pleasantness. 'I've only got four gifts to get in any case.'

A moment ago it had been just three. Her dad, Roger—in thanks for his kindness to the older man—and Daniel. But Cheryl was ruffling her feathers again and it was time that she did a bit of the same thing in return.

'But they're important ones,' she went on, 'for the four special men in my life.'

'And who might they be?' Jonas asked easily, with a guarded look in his eyes that belied his relaxed manner.

'My dad and Roger for starters,' she told him with equal nonchalance, 'and the other two shall be nameless.'

'I presume you're referring to patients?' the blonde leech said.

'Not at all. The hospital sees to that.'

Daniel was kicking an imaginary ball, his interest in the conversation waning. When he caught his father's glance on him he said, 'I'm hungry, Dad. Can we go and eat somewhere?'

'Count me out,' Sep said quickly. 'I'll see you all back at the apartment.'

'Me, too,' Gemma said with equal speed. 'I only wangled some free time this afternoon on the promise that I would do a couple of hours this evening.'

Before Jonas had the chance to make anything of that

she was waving goodbye and making for the nearest escalator with Sep just one step behind her.

'Do I take it that you don't want to play gooseberry either?' he asked with a lopsided grin.

If Gemma *had* been having any doubts about the relationship between Jonas and the young socialite, Sep's acceptance of it would have wiped them out.

Suddenly the Christmas lights seemed less bright, the special fever that comes with the anticipation of the season less frenetic, and she knew why.

She was going to play the two men in her life off against each other. Her father would be led to think that she was spending the eve of Christmas and the following festive day with Jonas and Daniel.

And if by any chance the charismatic plastic surgeon should repeat his casual invitation, she would tell him that she was going to the Isle of Man with her father and Roger.

In the event she would spend Christmas alone—a solitary situation maybe, but in the long run the least painful.

'I'm not with you,' she told Sep, as if she didn't understand what he was referring to.

'You and the doc?'

'And you and Cheryl?' she parried.

'Quits,' he conceded, and with a casual wave of the hand he loped off.

Gemma spent the weekend getting ready for her father's homecoming—changing sheets, vacuuming, dusting and stocking up on food from the nearby supermarket, with brief intervals when she stopped for a snack.

She'd picked up a small spruce on her way home on the Friday and her last job on Sunday night was to decorate it with the same treasured glass balls she'd had on her tree as a child.

By the time she'd finished she was tired and grubby and was about to take a shower when the doorbell rang.

She sighed. There had already been two lots of carol singers, bellowing lustily around the porch, and she'd felt guilty because she hadn't prepared the usual mince pies and coffee, but as most of them knew that Harry was in hospital and she was alone they'd gone on their way good-naturedly to the next port of call.

Whoever it was this time, they would have to go, she was thinking as she flew down the stairs. The shower was beckoning and she couldn't wait to get beneath it.

Her determination to send the caller packing lasted until the second she saw Jonas standing on the doorstep, his face ruddy from the cold, his dark eyes observing her questioningly.

Joy filled her at the sight of him, to be followed by dismay. Why did he have to come when she looked such a sight?

'J-Jonas!' she stammered, her breath frosting on the chill night air. 'What brings you here?'

'That's soon answered,' he replied easily. 'You, of course. Are you going to ask me in before I freeze to death?'

She stepped back. 'Yes, certainly. Another second and I would have been in the shower. As you can probably see by my dishevelled state, I've been having a very busy weekend, getting ready for Dad coming home.'

He neither agreed nor disagreed with her comment. Instead, he eased himself out of his heavy top coat and, as if completely at home in his surroundings, hung it on the coat-stand in the hall, then waited for her to lead the way into the sitting room.

He remained standing until she was seated and then took the chair opposite. As she fixed him with her wide hazel gaze he said, 'And when is your father being discharged?'

'Hopefully, next week.'

'So he'll have a fortnight before Christmas is upon him. That's one reason why I'm here, amongst others, but first I want to know why you rushed off in such a hurry on Friday afternoon. I didn't get to thank you for giving up your free time for Daniel.'

'It was my pleasure,' she said, looking down at her old trainers as if she'd been caught out in some misdemeanour.

'Maybe, but nevertheless it was good of you to go with them. If I'd known I would be back so early I would have gone with you.'

That brought her head up in protest. 'But you *were* back,' she argued stiffly. 'You and…she were in the store before us. You'd already made your purchases.'

'Cheryl had. She'd been there a long time before me. She called me on her mobile the second I arrived in the apartment to say that she'd seen the three of you in Harrods, so I called a taxi and came out to join you.'

He was frowning. 'Is there a problem?'

Gemma shook her head. She could hardly tell him that she'd been sick with envy when she'd seen them together.

'You're not still sore at me for asking you to marry me?'

'No, of course not.' She *wasn't* still sore. Sick at heart…yes.

'So we've cleared the air on that question?'

It was still a thick fog as far as she was concerned, but why take it further?

'Next question, Gemma. What have you sorted out for Christmas?'

'Dad is very keen to go to the Isle of Man.'

'With Roger Croft?'

'Mmm.'

'So that's it?'

She nodded, relief washing over her. Jonas was taking it

for granted that where her father went she would go. There had been no need for an outright lie.

'So you're not coming to us?'

'No. I'm afraid not.'

Another skilful evasion. She was being devious and knew it, but it was worth any amount of sidetracking to avoid spending part of Christmas as an onlooker while he and Cheryl furthered their relationship.

Maybe asking her to tag along had been Jonas's good deed for Christmas. His effort in aid of the needy. Yet when he'd heard that she had nothing planned he'd said that he and Daniel would be out on a limb, too. Who was he kidding?

'You haven't even considered the idea, have you?' he was asking stonily. 'You'd rather be with anyone other than Daniel and myself. Roger Croft! Sep!'

'And what about you?' she cried. 'Who would you rather be with? Certainly not me! I'm your Christmas charity case!'

'That remark is totally unjust! I hope you're seasick on the crossing!' he snapped. 'You deserve to be.'

'Thanks for your good wishes,' she flung back, 'but it would take more than a sail to the Isle of Man to upset *my* digestive tract.'

'Really? And what would it take to throw the rest of you off balance? Something like this?'

It took just two strides for him to imprison her in his arms, and as she looked up at him in startled amazement his eyes were telling her what his intentions were.

'I look awful!' she croaked inanely, but Jonas wasn't listening. He was yanking her hair out of the rubber band that had been holding it in place during her chores.

As it fell on to her shoulders in dark coils he ran his hands through the silken mass of it and sought her mouth with hard urgency.

The magic was there again. Gemma had known it would be and it was inevitable that she should respond. She would have been made of stone not to, yet all the time she was yielding to him the voice of uncertainty was making itself heard.

He knows how you feel about him and is taking pity on you, it was saying as she swayed beneath the avalanche of longing that his touch had triggered. Tonight of all nights when you're looking your worst! You've angered the man by not accepting his invitation and he's getting his own back. He might have lifted you up, but he will surely put you down just as quickly when it suits him.

'Stop it, Jonas!' she gasped, pushing him away. 'I never asked for you to do this. Say what you've come to say and go!'

He was breathing hard as if he'd been running but his voice was controlled enough as he told her, 'I've said all I came to say…or am ever likely to. You've made yourself quite clear. In future we'll stick to business, Gemma. That way neither of us are likely to hurt the other. Go to the Isle of Man for Christmas if that's what you want…and good luck to you!'

He wrenched the door open and without another word walked swiftly down the path. Gemma shivered as she watched him go, but it wasn't the cold of the winter night that was affecting her. It was tropical compared to the ice that seemed to be around her heart.

CHAPTER EIGHT

HAVING decided to keep any thoughts of the coming Christmas firmly to the back of her mind, the sight of a huge spruce being erected in the hospital forecourt the next morning did nothing to help Gemma keep to her decision.

Neither did the cheerful chatter of the nurses as they decorated the wards with the glitz and glitter that the season always called for.

Her father was also full of the Christmas spirit when she popped in to see him, making it abundantly clear that the thought of his fast-approaching discharge from the hospital and the proposed trip to the Isle of Man were giving him something to look forward to with relish.

But Harry wasn't so wrapped up in his own affairs that he didn't notice his daughter's lack of zest, and as his keen grey eyes noted her unusual listlessness and pallor he asked gruffly, 'What's wrong, Gemma, girl? You don't look like someone who's going to spend Christmas with the man of her dreams.'

She managed a smile. 'There's nothing wrong, Dad. I've just had a very busy weekend, that's all. I don't know when I'll get another one free so I've been catching up on some chores.'

'So it's nothing to do with Jonas Parry?'

'No, of course not. Everything is fine.'

It was fortunate that Jonas rarely went near Men's Surgical, otherwise her dad might mention the arrangements she was supposed to have made and that would have really put the cat amongst the pigeons.

She'd thought of telling him not to discuss Christmas

with Jonas if he saw him, but had known that the mere fact of asking him to keep quiet would have made Harry curious...and suspicious. So she was going to rely on Jonas's heavy workload and her father's apathy to the man she loved, to keep them apart.

When she arrived back on the wards a barrel-chested rugby player in the first bed called across good-humouredly, 'Morning, Doctor. Have you got a minute?'

'Yes, of course.' she said, going across to him. 'What can I do for you?'

Gemma was aware that silence had fallen on the ward and she wondered why. She didn't have to wait for an answer. The man, who had been admitted for skin grafts on his arm following a fire, pulled out a piece of mistletoe from under the sheets and kissed her firmly on the lips.

There was nothing offensive about the gesture. From the cheer that went up she guessed that there had been a dare of some sort. Joining into the spirit of the thing, she kissed him back, causing the uproar to increase.

'Whoops! Here's Jonas Parry!' someone said as the tomfoolery continued.

Gemma disentangled herself quickly and when she straightened up she found Jonas beside them, his face blanked of all expression and his voice flat as he said 'When you've finished entertaining the patients and staff Dr Bartlett, I'd like you to give me your opinion on a new admission.'

She was tucking her blouse back into her skirt and smoothing down her hair, as if it was the norm to be found in a clinch with a patient. Having no intentions of trying to justify it, she said with a calm that she was far from feeling, 'Yes, of course, Mr Parry. Where is the new admission?'

'So you haven't done your rounds yet?'

'It's my fault, Doctor,' the mistletoe man said with a

grin. 'They're long days in here and we're desperate for a bit of excitement. Some of the other patients dared me to kiss Dr Bartlett under the mistletoe and I didn't need to be asked twice.' His glance switched to Gemma who was squirming at the way the incident was being elaborated upon. 'I hope I didn't offend you.'

She shook her head. 'No. I took it in the spirit in which it was meant and now I must get back to work.'

'This way, then,' Jonas said with crisp coldness, and as James and Peter fell into step behind him, like a reluctant bridesmaid, she brought up the rear.

They stopped beside the bed of a three-year-old boy with a bluish-red birthmark along the side of his face and over part of his upper lip.

'I saw young Richard last week in Outpatients,' Jonas informed them. 'As you can see, he has a raised haemangioma which is causing him some problems as it has started to bleed every time he eats.

'Normally we wouldn't mess with it as these sorts of things often fade gradually over a period of years, but the fact that it partially covers the lip is creating a situation where we need to remove that area, if possible.

'Why do you think the birthmark has the bluish tinge to it, Dr Bartlett?' he asked suddenly.

Gemma swallowed hard. The day had not started well as far as she and Jonas were concerned. A wrong answer wasn't going to improve it. But she wasn't the *British Medical Encyclopaedia* in human form, neither was she yet one of the country's top plastic surgeons.

'Are we dealing with Sturge-Weber syndrome?'

She saw James's eyes widen and Peter's sardonic smile hovering and her spirits plummeted further, but surprisingly Jonas's reaction was an understanding nod, even though he was about to veto the suggestion.

'No, we're not,' he said, 'but I can see why you might

have thought so. Tests have shown that this youngster
skin problem isn't connected with brain abnormalitie
There is no weakness of the opposite side of the body
the skin blemishes, which there would be if it was th
Sturge-Weber syndrome. In his case it's simply a raise
haemangioma that will eventually disappear as he ge
older.

'Its bluish appearance is due to venous blood beneath th
discoloration which indicates that the affected tissues ar
deeper than those of a strawberry mark. There are variou
ways that I could attempt to remove the raised area from
the lip but I will probably resort to laser treatment in th
end.'

As the medical team moved away from the child's be
Jonas fell into step beside her and said in a low voice
'Never be afraid to say what you think, Gemma, eve
though you might be wrong. But we already know you d
that, don't we?'

'What?'

'Say what you think…and are sometimes wrong. Lik
last night, for instance, when you were falling over yoursel
to decide what my motives were in giving in to a perfectl
normal impulse.'

'What I said was true!' she protested with equal quiet
ness. 'You *do* see me as a charity case. I'm a woman who
comes into your working orbit and whom you feel bound
to keep an eye on for various reasons.'

'Maybe so…and maybe one of these days when you're
feeling less prickly I'll explain what those reasons are,
Jonas said with a quick glance to make sure they weren'
being overheard. 'In the meantime, we have work to do
Dr Bartlett.'

'Yes, Mr Parry,' she agreed with deferential docility as
Peter drew level with them, his keen eyes missing nothing

*   *   *

On the Friday of that week Gemma went late night shopping. Her outing with Daniel and Sep had been cut short when they'd come across Jonas and Cheryl and her purchases on that occasion had been nil.

This time it was different. There was no one to distract her. With the speed of the shopper who hasn't much time to spare she bought her father a new dressing-gown, Roger expensive aftershave, Daniel a game for his Playstation…and with a feeling of complete anticlimax a CD of Christmas music with trumpet solos for Jonas.

She'd stood, irresolute, in the shop for ages before choosing it, undecided as to whether she should make the gesture. He was wealthy, a man who must surely have everything he wanted. How would he look upon a small gift from an acquaintance, for that was all she was?

Would he think it an impertinence? Surely not. Hadn't he invited her to spend Christmas with them? For philanthropic reasons maybe, but he'd made the offer so a token of her regard shouldn't come amiss, she told herself convincingly, even though she hadn't been strictly truthful with him about her arrangements.

That same night something so worrying occurred that Christmas and every other coherent thought were wiped from her mind.

As she pulled up on the drive in front of the darkened house with her purchases on the seat beside her, a small figure stepped into the glare of the headlights.

Gemma's heart missed a beat. The mop of dark hair and the smooth olive skin were unmistakable and as she scrambled out of the car the first word on her lips was, 'Daniel!'

He was without a jacket and was shivering from the cold. 'What are you doing here?' she cried, adding before he could reply, 'Where's your father?'

'Dining with Grandad and Michaela,' he said, looking down at his feet.

His shoulders were hunched dejectedly, his hair damp from the night air, and as Gemma ushered him inside with all speed it was clear that something was not well in Daniel's secure world.

She waited until he was sitting in front of the fire with a mug of hot chocolate between his cold little hands and then asked gently, 'How did you get here, Daniel? And how did you know my address?'

'I came in a taxi,' he said with his head still bent, 'and I saw your address in the book on the hall table.'

'You could have rung me, rather than coming out on your own at this time of night.'

Sooner or later she was going to have to ask what was wrong, but for the moment she could wait.

'I did ring you,' he said, 'but you weren't in...and so I took some money out of my piggy bank and got a taxi. I told the driver that I'd been to a schoolfriend's party.'

'So does anyone know where you are?'

He shook his head.

'Where is Sep tonight?'

'He was in the shower when I came out.'

'And you didn't tell him where you were going?'

'No. I just wanted to get away.'

'Away from what?'

Instead of answering the question, he turned his head away and took a long drink from the mug.

'Away from what, Daniel?' she repeated.

'Away from her!' he cried, his voice rising.

Light was beginning to dawn. 'Who are we talking about? Cheryl?'

'Yes. She came just after Dad and the others had gone and while Sep was in the shower.'

'What did she do that was so dreadful that you had to run away?' she asked carefully.

'She tried to kiss me.'

Gemma hid a smile. She didn't like the girl but it wasn't a crime.

'That wasn't so awful, surely. Lots of people are like that.'

'It wasn't that,' he protested, with his bottom lip jutting out ominously. 'She said that she was going to be my new mother...and I hate her! As soon as she'd gone I ran away.'

'I see.'

That makes two of us who aren't happy, she thought, and what, for heaven's sake, is Jonas thinking of, allowing Cheryl to break that sort of news to his son in such a manner?

Anger was ripping through her, but surmounting it was the need to let Sep know that Daniel was safe. The amiable au pair would be frantic when he found the boy missing.

As if reading her mind, Daniel stared up at her defiantly. 'I'm not going home,' he said. 'I want to stay here with you.'

'That's something we can talk about in the morning,' she said soothingly, 'but for now I have to let Sep know where you are. He'll never think of coming here to look for you.'

'All right,' he agreed reluctantly, 'but ask him to tell Dad that I'm not coming home.'

'Very well,' she agreed gravely.

As Gemma picked up the phone to ring the Pimlico apartment her heart was twisting. What Daniel had told her made it clear that the relationship between Jonas and Cheryl was an established fact. It was too bad that the boy and herself, both loving Jonas so dearly, should discover the seriousness of the commitment in such a way.

One thing was for sure. She would never hold him in high regard again. For him to have allowed the confident young beautician to break such disturbing news to his son in such a casual manner was unforgivable.

That was all that mattered at the moment. The effect of the news upon herself was something that would have to be shelved until Daniel had been comforted and had regained his confidence.

'Yes?' a voice barked in her ear, and Gemma knew that it was not Sep at the other end of the line.

'It's Gemma here,' she said, her voice tightening.

'I can't talk now,' he said raggedly. 'I've just come in and found that Daniel is missing!'

'Was.'

'What?'

'He's here with me. I found him waiting in the drive when I got back from shopping.'

There was a stunned silence and she thought stonily. You've asked for this, Jonas.

'Thank God!' he breathed. 'I was just about to ring the police. I'll come and get him.'

'No! He doesn't want you to. Not tonight, anyway.'

There was total amazement in his voice as he asked, 'Why, for heaven's sake?'

'That's something you need to ask your fiancée.'

'My fiancée?'

'That's what I said.'

'This is ridiculous!'

'Isn't it just? However, the fact remains that Daniel wants to stay with me tonight. Do you trust me with him?'

'Yes, of course I do!' he snapped, 'but—'

'But nothing,' Gemma told him grimly. 'We'll talk to you tomorrow. As it's Saturday and I'm off duty until lunchtime, he can sleep late, and in the meantime you can tell Miss Tactless that small children should be handled with care when it comes to the foundations of their young lives being threatened.'

'If it was anyone else rambling on like this I would have serious doubts about their sanity,' Jonas growled, 'but as it's you...'

'You'll give me the benefit of the doubt?'

'Mmm, and now fetch my son to the phone to say goodnight. I won't ask him what all this is about, but tomorrow I shall be requiring some answers from you both.'

'The answers need to come from you, Jonas...and you're right not to pressure him now. Daniel is tired and upset. Just say goodnight and leave him to me.'

'Night, Dad,' Daniel mumbled into the receiver when she handed it to him, then thrust it quickly back into her hand.

He went back to his place by the fire, leaving Jonas to exclaim, 'What *is* going on?'

'Leave it for now,' Gemma suggested in a gentler tone. 'It's time your son was tucked up in bed.'

An hour later she stood looking down at Daniel. The strain had left his face and in sleep he was tranquil and adorable to the eye.

She had changed the sheets on her bed for him and had made up the sofa for herself. It was comfortable enough, and even if it hadn't been she would have been prepared to sleep on the clothesline rather than allow Jonas's son to suffer any discomfort.

There was an angry sort of sadness churning around inside her, made up of disillusion, despair and fury at the careless way that a small boy's life had been turned upside down.

Jonas must be blind, she thought bitterly as she lay curled up on the couch through the long night. He could have any woman he wanted and he had to choose a brassy-haired opportunist.

When she surfaced the next morning, after finally slipping into sleep as a wintry dawn broke, Gemma was conscious of someone standing over her, and when she opened her eyes she found Daniel looking down at her.

'You look just as nice when you wake up as the rest of the time,' he remarked.

She laughed sleepily, flexing cramped neck muscles as she did so. 'I doubt it. Are you hungry?'

'Yes.'

'Right. Then while you watch the Saturday morning cartoons I'll rustle us up some breakfast.'

They'd eaten and were curled up on the couch together when there was a knock on the kitchen door and Jonas came striding in.

'Very cosy for some,' he commented drily, 'especially as there are those of us whose nerve ends are rather tattered this morning.'

Gemma got to her feet, tightening the belt of a heavy silk robe as she did so.

'A certain young man wasn't exactly happy either when he arrived here last night.'

She motioned for Daniel to go into the kitchen and, having closed the door behind her, said tartly, 'Do you think so little of your son that you would allow someone else to tell him that you are about to remarry? How could you?'

'You're rambling on again.' he said accusingly. 'Instead of taking it for granted that I know what you are talking about, why don't you explain?'

'I wouldn't have thought it necessary,' she snarled, 'but certainly...if you insist. Take a seat.'

'No. I'll stand.'

'Suit yourself.'

'I intend to. So?'

'Daniel ran away last night because your friend Cheryl told him that she was to be his new mother. It's as simple as that. Between the pair of you he could have come to great harm.'

'What do you mean—between the pair of us?' he questioned icily. 'I left the house last night in the knowledge that my son was happy and safe...and that situation shouldn't have changed.

'The fact that it did certainly wasn't my fault. I shall have strong words with that woman when next we meet...and in the meantime I will make sure that whatever is troubling my son is sorted out. I would never knowingly cause him distress.'

'Short of giving her the elbow?' she asked with casual sweetness.

'That's for me to decide and for you to find out,' he said abruptly. 'Thank you for looking after Dan. I'll be in touch.'

'Not if I see you first,' she flashed back with continuing flippancy as tears threatened.

He tutted impatiently and, turning on his heel went into the kitchen. 'Let's go home, shall we, Danny boy?' he said, and when Gemma dredged up a smile and nodded her agreement the boy got reluctantly to his feet.

'Will she be there?' he asked.

'No. *She* won't be there,' his father said, and on that promise they went.

Gemma slumped down onto the couch and gazed bleakly out onto the winter morning. Jonas hadn't denied the engagement, she thought wretchedly. He'd merely said he would have words with Mighty Mouth.

Nothing would change, except that Daniel would be gentled into the new arrangement in such a way that it didn't cause distress...initially. But unless the bride-to-be underwent a big change of personality Daniel would soon be miserable, and Gemma couldn't bear the thought of his security being threatened.

The only good thing to come out of it would be that her concern for the boy might take the edge off her own misery, and almost as if the fates also had that matter in hand the phone rang.

She answered it listlessly and a voice at the other end informed her that her father was on the point of being discharged and would she please come and get him?

Gemma had no time to brood during the rest of the day. No sooner had she got Harry settled back home than it was time to do her shift at the hospital.

Her father was sitting blissfully in his favourite chair in front of the TV when she left, with a snack laid out on a nearby table and the stick he'd been relying on since the accident within reach.

'Don't worry about me,' he told her. 'Roger knows I'm being discharged today and that you're working. He's promised to come round to keep an eye on me.' His smile was a bright beam as he went on to say, 'We'll be planning our trip to the Isle of Man. Now that I'm home he can book the flights.'

Gemma's heart warmed at his enthusiasm. It was worth a few white lies if it made her father happy. He looked across at her and said, 'You're still sorted, I hope.'

She continued with the deception. 'Yes, of course. Everything is arranged for me to spend what leave I'm due with Jonas and Daniel. Once I've seen you off at the airport I'll go straight there.'

'We can't go until later in the day of Christmas Eve,' Harry said. 'Roger has a surgery in the morning. I expect he'll try for a flight in the late afternoon.'

He eyed her thoughtfully. 'So you still think you're in love with the plastic surgeon?'

Gemma sighed. She could answer that question truthfully. Disillusioned, cheesed-off, jealous she might be, but it didn't make any difference to the fact that Jonas made her blood heat, her heart beat faster and controlled her every waking thought.

'I don't "think" I'm in love with Jonas,' she told him. 'I *know* I'm in love with him. Nothing is going to change that.'

She'd said it with smiling firmness but a few minutes later as she wove in and out of the Saturday traffic she couldn't raise a smile to save her life.

How was Daniel feeling? she wondered. Was he any happier? Jonas loved him dearly and by now would have talked to him, but how was the boy going to cope in the long term?

It was James's weekend off, but Peter was there when she got to the hospital. His tweed jacket and trousers contrasting sharply with her white hospital coat.

'I'm off in an hour,' he said as if she'd questioned his attire. 'Are you up to holding the fort?'

'Depends how heavy it is.'

'Ha. Ha.'

'If you're pointing out that I'm the only doctor on call, yes, I can cope, just as long as Accident and Emergency don't start taking them in droves. Where will you be if they do?' she teased.

'Nowhere you'll be able to reach me,' he said with a grin. 'I'm going Christmas shopping with the wife. I don't know which I fancy less. Working on a Saturday afternoon or being trampled in the crush around the shops. At least it doesn't cost me anything when I'm working.'

He'd made no mention of being aware that their superior was about to remarry and, knowing Peter's fondness for gossip and giving anything of interest a quick stir, she could only conclude that Jonas was keeping his private affairs strictly to himself.

That being the case, there was no way that *she* was going

to spread the story around the hospital as once it became common knowledge the grapevine would have a field day.

Thank goodness her feelings for Jonas weren't common knowledge either. That would have been just too embarrassing for words.

Although health problems and accidents weren't necessarily restricted to weekdays, there was always a less fraught atmosphere on the wards at weekends, and it was early evening before any kind of crisis presented itself.

A message came through to the ward, requesting that the doctor on call make his or her way to Accident and Emergency with all speed, and when Gemma got there she had cause to remember her laughing comment to Peter. Injured members of the public *were* being brought to the hospital in droves!

'Coach crash!' the sister on the unit said briefly as she dashed past her to get to the stretcher that was just arriving.

'Paramedics at the scene report many facial injuries and fractures. We're having to call on all medical personnel who can be spared. It's going to be a long night. I don't suppose that Jonas Parry is around?'

Gemma shook her head. Neither were Peter or James. She was the only one from their unit who was available.

An elderly registrar who had heard the sister's comments said, 'We're putting a call out for all off-duty staff to report in. That's how serious it is. In the meantime, we've got sixteen injured on their way, with more to come, and three already admitted.'

He looked around him. 'Some of those already in here will have to be taken to the wards. Otherwise we'll have no room for the new arrivals.'

Gemma was already bending over the nearest stretcher on which an elderly man lay unconscious, his head and face bloodstained and his legs strapped together to prevent further displacement of broken bones.

'Right. Let's get him onto a bed,' she said to the paramedics who had just brought him in, 'and he needs to be on his side. With these kind of injuries there could be intra-oral bleeding.'

She hadn't forgotten how Sally Graham had almost died with airway obstruction from the looseness of her tongue and displaced teeth.

They lifted him carefully, using a passing nurse to assist them in holding the four corners of the sheet he was lying on as they transferred him from the stretcher.

Once he was on the bed Gemma brought his tongue forward and cleaned the debris from his mouth. While she was working on him the man gave a feeble groan and a few seconds later he opened his eyes.

'Where's my wife?' he asked weakly. 'Where Ellie?'

Gemma eyed the paramedics questioningly and one of them said, 'She was in the ambulance behind us. They were in the front seat.'

'Your wife is on her way here,' she told him gently, 'and while you're waiting for her to arrive we're going to clean you up and have a look at your legs.'

The paramedics had already left to go back to the scene of the accident, and when the man's trouser legs were cut away it was clear that he had suffered multiple fractures.

'I'm sending him to X-Ray,' she told the nurse who was gently sponging his face, 'for facial and leg fractures.'

After that there seemed to be no end to stitching, X-rays and hurried dashes to Theatre for the busy staff, and in the middle of it all Gemma had to find time to ring her father to explain that she would be delayed.

Roger answered the phone and for once she was glad to hear his voice. 'I'll stay until you come home,' he offered with just the slightest note of censure in his voice. 'We can't leave your dad on his own on his first night out of hospital.'

She thanked him awkwardly, wishing that it had been someone else she'd had to ask a favour of, and hurried back to the emergency area.

On this dark winter's night the world seemed to be full of pain and problems. This was where she was needed the most, but Roger had made her feel guilty at not being with her father.

If the hospital had told her in advance that he would be home today she might have been able to get the time off, but the last time she'd asked they hadn't known when he would be discharged.

Feeling tired and lonely, she put her aching head against the cold brick of the wall beside the door of the accident area and allowed herself a brief moment's respite.

'Gemma!' Jonas's voice said suddenly from behind. 'What's wrong?'

He saw her slender shoulders stiffen and then she turned slowly to face him. Her face white in the light of a flitting moon, her eyes dark and luminous.

'Nothing,' she said softly. 'Nothing is wrong...now.' The last word had been said so quietly that it was like a sigh on the wind, and he wondered if he'd imagined it.

'They sent for me,' he explained, 'but I was out and didn't get the message until close on midnight.' He smiled and his teeth gleamed whitely in the darkness. 'However, I'm here now. So shall we go inside and join the fray?'

She nodded mutely. It wasn't the moment to be conjecturing about where he'd been and with whom. It was sufficient that he was here, ready to offer his skills and cool competence to those who desperately needed them.

It was almost daylight by the time Gemma was ready to leave. Jonas had disappeared into Theatre the moment they'd gone inside. She had been treating those waiting to be operated on, or those whose injuries were not quite so severe, and now she was about to go home, exhausted but satisfied that she'd been able to contribute to an emergency which had been on a bigger scale than she'd ever encountered before.

A grey December day was just becoming visible as she paused on the steps outside the hospital's main entrance. Tired as she was, there were two reasons why she wasn't rushing home.

The first was because Roger would still be there if he'd kept his promise to stay with her father until she got back, the second because Jonas was still ensconced in Theatre and, separate as their private lives might be, she longed to see him, if only for a moment, before she went home.

Her wish was granted. As Gemma started to walk slowly down the flight of stone steps she heard the huge swing doors swish open behind her and even as her step faltered she heard him call her name from behind for a second time.

As he drew level he flexed his shoulders and then stretched out his arms. 'Whew! It's been a long night!' he said with a wry smile, 'and even longer for you. You've been here since yesterday lunchtime, haven't you?'

She gave a tired nod. 'Yes. I'd no sooner brought Dad home than I was leaving him, which was bad enough when I thought it was only for a few hours. I never expected it to be this long.'

Jonas was eyeing her in concern, noting the dark shadows beneath her eyes, the lines of fatigue that were draining her clear skin of its beauty, and he chided himself for not sending her home earlier. She had looked exhausted when he'd found her outside the emergency ward and that had been hours ago, and for her to have the added worry about her father being alone...

'Roger Croft is with Dad,' she told him, as if reading his thoughts. 'He kindly offered to keep him company when he knew I was going to be delayed.'

'Ah, yes,' he said slowly. 'The three of you are very good friends, aren't you? In fact, you're spending Christmas together if I remember rightly.'

He had no idea how much she would have liked to have denied that, Gemma thought as a cold wind stung her cheeks, but it was too late now to admit she hadn't been truthful with him…and would he care if she did come clean?

'Yes, that's right,' she agreed blandly. 'Christmas can't come quickly enough.' And if that wasn't the biggest whopper of all, she didn't know what was.

They were on the forecourt now, making their way to their cars, and Jonas said gravely, 'I'm glad that you're looking forward to it, Gemma. You deserve to be happy.' As desolate tears began to prick he bent and kissed her cheek.

The sudden action made her swivel towards him and their mouths met in what was almost a butterfly kiss. The unexpected contact rocked her on her feet.

Within seconds they were holding each other with a fierce sort of hunger. Gemma's mouth was saying the words that had always stuck in her throat. Her body moulding itself to his with the sensual longing of a woman who desired a man completely.

The long night forgotten, it was as if renewed zest was flowing through her. A car hooter sounded almost under their noses, and when, startled and bemused, she dragged herself out of Jonas's arms she saw Roger Croft's unsmiling face observing them.

'I couldn't stay with your father any longer,' he informed her coldly. 'I've been called out to a seriously ill patient.'

On that sour note he turned his car and went, leaving Jonas with a strange smile on his face and Gemma weak with embarrassment.

She'd deserved Roger's disapproval, she thought as she

hugged her long winter coat around her miserably. He had been left to look after her father. With good reason, admittedly, but he'd been lumbered nevertheless.

And as for Jonas, well, she'd been limp and unresisting once again.

Between the two of them her mind was in chaos and when Jonas made no move to detain her as she continued to walk towards her car Gemma accepted that what to her had been a moment of sweet madness, to him had been just a quick kiss and cuddle with someone that he knew he could pick up and put down whenever he felt like it.

CHAPTER NINE

THE rest of Sunday seemed to fly by and Gemma thought ruefully that Monday morning would be upon her before she'd had time to recover from the trauma of Saturday night.

She did manage a couple of hours' sleep in the afternoon, after she had filled her father in with the happenings that had caused her to be absent for so long.

He'd sighed when she'd finished describing the aftermath of the coach crash. 'It's not the same since I retired. I really miss being involved in the NHS. I know that the humble GP isn't on the same level as Jonas Parry and an up-and-coming young doctor like yourself, but we did have our moments down at the practice.'

Gemma had patted his weatherbeaten cheek gently. 'Hospital staff have the greatest respect for the family doctor. He or she is just as important in health care as we are. And,' she told him smilingly, 'don't forget that you *have* been involved with the NHS over the last few weeks. From the other side of the fence maybe, but involved nevertheless.'

'Aye,' he'd agreed sombrely. 'I went down like the Titanic. I was lucky that I didn't harm myself more than I did, but here I am—' his voice lifted '—and I'm going away for Christmas for the fist time in my life.'

She hadn't taken him up on that comment. Least said, soonest mended, but Harry wasn't going to let it drop.

'Roger tells me that he's found somebody else,' he said with a touch of tetchiness. 'One of the receptionists at the surgery. You've kept him hanging on too long.'

'I've never given him any cause to think I cared for him,' she protested. 'Any "hanging on" has been of his own doing.' The implications of this new development hit her. 'Is she going to the Isle of Man as well?'

He shook his head. 'No. He's only known her a couple of weeks, and in any case she'd already made arrangements to go to Majorca for Christmas.'

Oh, what a tangled web! Gemma had thought as she'd snuggled down beneath the covers of her virginal bed in the early afternoon. Anything but deceitful by nature, the role she had cast for herself sat uneasily upon her shoulders.

Roger came early in the evening to pick up a book he'd left behind, or so he said, and Gemma wondered if he would have any comments to make about their meeting on the hospital car park early that morning.

It seemed that he hadn't, or at least if he had he was keeping them to himself for the time being. As she listened to the two men talking Gemma wished she could have fallen in love with someone like him, whose private life was uncomplicated, with no previous marriages that had left him hurt and angry, who was an open book when it came to integrity...and without a single ounce of charisma!

When she went to the door with him as he was leaving, he said awkwardly, 'I'm seeing someone else. Has your dad told you?'

She nodded. 'Yes. I hope that it works out for you.' And because his relationship with some strange woman was an unknown quantity, she followed it by saying carefully, 'You *will* look after Dad while you're away, won't you? He's really looking forward to the break.'

'I'm not going to neglect your dad because his daughter isn't interested in me,' he told her drily. 'I'd hoped that you thought better of me than that.'

'I do,' she'd assured him, 'but at the moment my mind and my life seem to be in complete confusion.'

'Enjoy your Christmas, Gemma,' he said, ignoring her plea for understanding as he turned to go.

'I'll try,' she promised limply.

At half past eight the phone rang and when she picked it up Gemma was surprised to hear Daniel's voice on the line.

'Gemma?' he said.

'Yes, I'm here,' she said softly.

'Would you like to come to the theatre with us?'

'Er…what are you going to see?'

'*Scrooge*. Dad said to ring and ask if you'd like to join us.'

'Why didn't he ask me himself?' she questioned mildly, having no wish to involve Daniel in the complexities of her relationship with his father.

'He said that you would say no if *he* asked you.'

'And knowing that you are one of my very favourite people, he decided that I wouldn't be able to refuse *you*?'

'Something like that, I suppose.'

'In that case…yes, I would love to go to the theatre, providing I'm not on duty at the hospital. I'm not like your dad who can please himself, you know. I have to do as I'm told. When is it to be?'

'Next Friday.'

She smiled into the mouthpiece. 'It so happens that I'm free on that night.' Was it possible that Jonas had known that?

'Good,' he said happily. 'And guess what?'

'What?'

'We might be moving house. Dad is going to view some properties next week.'

'Where?' she croaked, praying that Jonas wasn't intending to change jobs as well as houses.

'Somewhere on the Thames,' he said vaguely. 'I want a big garden and Dad wants a view.'

'I see,' she said slowly as some of the tension left her. At least they weren't going to move far. Anyway, what had it to do with her if they did?

Daniel had just said that he wanted a big garden. Maybe Jonas did too...for little Cheryls to play in while he and she gazed out over the river.

'So I'll see you on Friday?' Daniel said into the silence.

'Indeed you will,' she promised and, with the same train of thought persisting, told herself that she'd probably been asked along as company for Daniel while the other two were engrossed in each other.

On Monday morning Gemma was surprised to hear from Peter that Jonas had invited his immediate staff out for a meal that evening.

'This guy certainly is different,' he said with begrudging admiration. 'We don't usually get invited out by the élite, although it's a bit short notice.'

Gemma nodded, in agreement with all three points he'd raised. Jonas *was* different—as far as she was concerned, anyway. And they weren't usually invited out by the consultants. Added to which, it *was* short notice. But it appeared that everyone invited was intending to be there if possible.

Jonas was in Theatre most of the day, and by the time Gemma was ready to go home to change for the evening ahead there had been no sign of him.

However, she consoled herself with the thought that unlike most of her evenings this one showed promise. A meal at the end of a busy working day, with her colleagues *and* Jonas, was not to be sneezed at.

By the time she'd prepared her father's evening meal, and seen him settled comfortably in front of the television, there wasn't much time to spare, but it was enough.

When she came downstairs in a black calf-length dress,

with sheer stockings and high-heeled shoes, her hair held back with a silver clip that matched her jewellery, and an unmistakable glow about her, Harry's eyes misted.

'I hope Jonas Parry realises that he's a very lucky man,' he said gruffly, hiding his emotion.

'There are a few of us dining together,' Gemma explained, 'It isn't an intimate dinner for two.'

'Maybe, but he'll be wishing it was when he sees you.'

She shook her head. If he only knew! But the mirror in her bedroom *had* reflected a slender brunette dressed with tasteful elegance and, whatever Jonas might think when he saw her, Gemma's spirits were high.

They faltered somewhat when she realised that she was the last to arrive and that all eyes were upon her as she walked into the restaurant. One pair in particular were observing her with a dark intensity that made her cheeks warm, and as Jonas came forward to welcome her he said in a low voice, 'You are so beautiful.'

There was no time to let him see that he'd made her heart sing. The rest of the party was clustering around them and the head waiter was approaching to say that their table was ready.

Whether by accident or design, she wasn't sure, Gemma found herself seated next to Jonas, with James on the other side, but if she'd expected further expressions of approval she was to be disappointed.

'What have you done with your father tonight?' he asked as they ate the excellent food and drank the wines served with it.

'Left him tucked up in front of the television with a supper tray...which means that I mustn't be late home. Dad only came out of hospital a couple of days ago, and although he's recovering very well I feel he hasn't seen all that much of me since.'

He nodded his dark head understandingly. 'I think domestic arrangements will have most of us arriving home at an early hour. I've left Daniel with Sep, and most of the nurses here have had to dash around finding child-minders with my invitation being a last-minute affair.'

'Yes, why was that?' she questioned. 'You're normally so highly organised.'

His smile was wry. 'You think so? I'll give you two possible reasons and you can take your pick. One is because I am so busy that it was only yesterday that I discovered I had a free night.'

'And the other?'

'That an impromptu occasion such as this might give me the chance to spend some prime time with a certain junior doctor.'

Gemma gazed at him in surprise, expecting to see amusement in his expression, but his face was grave, the eyes holding hers waiting for her reaction.

Peter got to his feet at that second, glass in hand, a smile on his face for once. Gazing around him at the friends and colleagues who had blissfully put the thought of health care behind them for a few hours, he began to propose a toast.

'To Jonas Parry, our host,' he said, 'May he continue saving faces and other parts of the anatomy in the way that only he can.' As laughter rippled around the table he added, 'Along with our invaluable help, of course.'

As Jonas raised his glass in smiling salute it was a sign that the evening was almost over and their moment had gone, just like all the others, but what had she expected in a room full of people?

Taxis were coming and going as the diners made their departures, and as Gemma waited, with James by her side, Jonas came towards them.

'Shall we share a cab, Gemma?' he suggested.

As if the devil were well and truly at her elbow James chipped in, 'She can come with me, Jonas. We're going in the same direction.' Before she could protest he had taken her arm and was steering her towards the taxi that had just pulled up in front of them.

'Wait a moment!' Jonas called after them.

But James was tucking her into the back seat of the cab and as he settled down beside her it pulled away. Gemma twisted round for a last glimpse of Jonas through the back window. He was standing motionless on the pavement, a tall figure in a dark evening suit, with his face in shadow and his thoughts...what were they?

The same as hers? Frustrated? Filled with longing? Or those of a man who had done the right thing by those beneath him and had been prepared to make sure that one of the loose cannons amongst them got safely home?

If she'd arrived home with less sparkle than when she'd left, her father hadn't noticed.

'I've had my supper,' he'd said sleepily when she'd appeared beside him. 'I'm off to bed, and it wouldn't do you any harm to do the same. You've had an exhausting time of late. Or are you going to have something to warm you up first?'

He couldn't have guessed how appealing that suggestion had been, Gemma thought as she lay listening to her father's gentle snores rippling through from the next room, but it wasn't milk and biscuits she had in mind, and why, for goodness' sake, wasn't she doing something about it, instead of letting Jonas waste himself on a certain spoiled beautician?

The answer was there almost before she'd posed the question. She wasn't going to throw herself where she wasn't wanted...she had too much pride and dignity.

But pride and dignity were cold bedfellows. They didn't make the blood heat or the senses leap.

*   *   *

The next morning Peter was taking the outpatients clinic, with Gemma assisting. He'd drunk a lot the night before and wasn't in the best of moods, but as she wasn't exactly feeling on top of the world herself she didn't mind.

Their first patient was Mary Spencer, a retired headmistress whose foot had almost been severed some weeks previously by a falling stone gatepost in the local park.

She had been rushed into Accident and Emergency where immediate surgery had been required on damaged tendons and splintered bones, and now she was attending Outpatients for further treatment on an area of exposed bone on her ankle.

After both doctors had examined the injured foot Peter said, 'We're going to have to do a skin graft, Mrs Spencer.' Turning to Gemma, he said, 'Don't you agree, Dr Bartlett?'

She eyed him in some surprise. It wasn't like Peter to ask for her opinion. Jonas might, but not the sardonic registrar. Yet she was relieved that he had done, because if he hadn't she would have had to speak up as she didn't agree with what he'd said.

'Er...no, I'm afraid I don't,' she said quietly, aware of the patient's intent gaze. 'I feel that a skin flap would give better results than a graft.'

He waved a gracious hand in her direction. 'Do carry on,' he invited, but the look in his eyes didn't match the gesture.

Gemma swallowed. In for a penny, in for a pound!

'A skin flap will retain its blood supply when the blood vessels from the donor site are attached to the affected area by microsurgery...*and* it is less likely to contract when healing commences, along with an improved cosmetic appearance.'

She felt as if she was laying it on thick, but he *had* asked her what she thought.

'Thank you,' he said with a steely smile. Turning back

to the patient, he said, 'Dr Bartlett is a trainee on the unit and as such I have to assess her knowledge on these matters. As it turned out she didn't fall into the little trap that I had set for her.'

'A skin flap it will be, Mrs. Spencer. Performed either by myself or Mr Parry, our senior consultant. You will be hearing from us in the very near future.'

As the woman got up to go, leaning heavily on her stick, there was a grain of satisfaction for an angry Gemma. 'Thank you, Doctor,' she said, looking directly at her, and with a long, level look at the registrar she hobbled out.

The moment the door had closed behind her Peter said furiously, 'Don't ever do that to me again, Miss Smarty Pants! You made me look a complete fool!'

'You managed that all by yourself,' she said with a calmness she was far from feeling. 'You *did* ask me for my opinion. Jonas does the same thing sometimes and *he* wouldn't expect me to say something I didn't mean.'

'What's going on here?' Jonas's voice said tightly from the doorway. 'Your voices can be heard all over the hospital!'

As they swung round to face him the discomfited registrar said smoothly, 'I was just putting Dr Bartlett right on one or two things.'

'Such as?'

'Patient protocol.'

'I see. And what have *you* to say, Gemma?'

There was a lot she could have said, such as she was being blamed for someone else's inefficiency, had been made to look small in front of a patient *and* had been spoken to with great rudeness, but there was no way she was going to lower herself to Peter's level.

He was eyeing her warily, anxiety behind his smooth bravado, but he needn't have worried. If Jonas was going to take it further he could do so. She wasn't going to say anything, but any future dealings she had with Peter would be kept to a minimum. He was a liar and a coward.

Jonas was waiting for her answer and when it came his expression didn't change.

'Nothing, I'm afraid. Except that I'm sorry if we've disrupted the clinic.'

'I see. Well, perhaps you'll present yourself at my office after lunch, Dr Bartlett.' And on that solemn summons he went.

For the rest of the morning the two doctors worked in stilted harmony, with Gemma praying that all those they still had to see might have health problems that wouldn't lead to further strife between herself and the acerbic registrar.

'And what was all that about?' Jonas asked when she presented herself at his office as requested.

'I'd rather not say,' she told him.

'That's no answer, Gemma. The pair of you were almost brawling in the middle of the clinic! Had French been making a pass at you?'

She stared at him. 'No. I'd be the last person he'd do that to.'

'And why is that?'

'He thinks I'm teacher's pet.'

A smile hovered around his mouth. 'Myself being the teacher?

'Yes.'

'So what was the problem then?'

His voice had softened but she sensed he wasn't going to give up. Some sort of explanation would have to be offered.

'It was a dispute about a patient's treatment, that's all.'

His face cleared. 'You're saying that French was being his usual arrogant self?'

The answer to that was a simple 'yes' but there was no way she was going to say it and so she stayed mute.

'I should have known that you wouldn't behave like that for no reason,' he conceded. 'But the treatment of our patients is what we are all here for and we aren't paid to make mistakes.

'It's clear that you aren't prepared to give me the details, which convinces me that no actual harm was done but do, please, bear in mind that those who come to us for help are the ones that matter, not staff members engaged in an internal squabble.'

Gemma nodded. She didn't need to be reminded of what their function was. She agreed entirely with what Jonas was saying, but in this instance the chastisement was undeserved. Peter was the culprit, but because he was such a slippery customer he had wriggled his way out of it.

Jonas was waiting for her to say something, but she merely asked stiffly, 'Is that it? Can I go?'

He didn't reply. Instead, he had a question of his own. 'Did you get home safely last night?'

'There is no one I'd be safer with than James,' she told him drily.

'Agreed. But he *was* in rather a hurry to get you out of my clutches.'

'I don't think that even occurred to him.' She was smiling now. 'He would be rushing to get home to his wife. He worships her. I feel quite envious sometimes when he speaks of her so tenderly.'

'Tenderness is a precious commodity,' Jonas said softly, walking round the desk to stand beside her. 'Do you have any for me, Gemma? Your father once said you did, but if you have you keep it well hidden. I know that you have it for my son. Daniel's fondness for you is because he senses it, but where have I gone wrong?'

Where had he gone wrong? Was the man blind? He had

only to reach out and touch her and she melted with long-ing. He was doing it now, taking her gently by her forearms and pulling her close, so close that her breasts were crushed against him and she could feel his heart beating with strong rhythmic thuds.

As she looked up at him the thought came that if Jonas wanted tenderness he could have it. There was a great un-plumbed well of it inside her and, bringing his head down to hers with gentle fingers, she kissed his lips, his cheeks, the dark brows above surprised eyes, the hollow of his throat, and would have gone on from there if a pert voice hadn't broken into the dreamland she was creating.

It belonged to Cheryl. She was in the outer office, asking Jonas's secretary if he was available. He groaned and put Gemma gently from him.

'My "step-aunt" and I have an appointment,' he ex-plained. 'Last night it was James Brice butting in and today it's—'

'Daniel's would-be mother?' she finished off for him in a voice that was as flat as the floor beneath her feet.

'It's Dr Bartlett, isn't it?' Cheryl said sweetly as Gemma walked past on her way out. 'If Jonas has retired by the time I need a face-lift, I'll bear you in mind.'

He was rolling his eyes heavenwards but there was no anger in them, and as Cheryl steamed through the door of the outer office Gemma was vowing that never again would she let the man near her.

If he was looking for tenderness he was looking in the wrong place where Cheryl was concerned. She doubted if that one knew the meaning of the word!

On Friday night Gemma dressed for her outing to the the-atre with mixed feelings. In spite of her frustrations with regard to Jonas and herself and the gloom they evoked in her, she couldn't help a feeling of pleasurable anticipation at the thought of spending some time with father and son.

To be in the company of the blonde appendage was another matter but, circumstances being what they were, she was going to have to grin and bear it if she wanted to be with Jonas and Daniel.

In a gold beaded top and a long skirt of warm green silk she felt that she looked festive without being too colourful, and on impulse she fastened her hair up with two gold combs.

When she stepped back to view the effect she was satisfied. 'Top that if you can, Miss Mighty Mouth,' she said challengingly, but the other girl already had. She'd got Jonas.

She was ready with minutes to spare and when her father saw her he said, 'Once again you look good enough to eat. Just how serious is this thing between the two of you?'

'We're just friends, that's all.'

That wasn't a lie. They *were* just friends.

Harry sighed. 'I sense that's it's more than that, on your part anyway. Do you have to be involved with a second-hand Joe…with encumbrances?'

'His name is Jonas…and if you're referring to his son as an encumbrance, don't. Daniel is delightful.'

The sound of a car engine outside brought the discussion to an end.

'They're here now,' she told him, and after giving him a quick hug she picked up her evening bag. 'Don't worry about me, Dad. I know what I'm doing.' He gave a reluctant nod and she was glad he couldn't see her expression as she turned away.

'You look lovely,' Daniel said as she got into the car, and immediately went bright red.

Jonas laughed. 'You have made an impression on this young man. He wouldn't usually notice if those around him vere dressed in sackcloth...and he's quite right. You are a ight to behold, Gemma Bartlett.'

'Thank you,' she said quietly. Having no wish for the vening to start on a high that would almost certainly not ast, she asked, 'Where's Cheryl?'

Daniel grinned up at her. 'She couldn't come.'

The urge to cry Yippee! was strong but she managed to keep a straight face, which became even straighter as it lawned on her that she'd been included in the visit to the heatre to use up a spare ticket.

'So I'm filling the gap,' she said, directing the question t the man in the driving seat.

He eyed her briefly. 'No. You aren't.'

Gemma turned her head away. Did he really expect her o believe that?

As they made their way through the jostling crowd in he theatre foyer Gemma couldn't help imagining that they vere a family out for the night. Doting parents and a small live-skinned boy.

One of them was already filling the role, and the other ne could have been if she'd accepted a loveless proposal f marriage.

Supposing she had. Where would it have left the absent Cheryl? In the same position as herself? On the sidelines?

From what she'd seen of her, that wouldn't have suited. he girl was bossy and demanding. Why didn't the beau- ful Michaela take her in hand?

The production of *Scrooge*, presented to a full house, was xcellent. Both Gemma's and Daniel's eyes were riveted to he stage, but there seemed to be a lesser degree of interest n Jonas's part and a few times she found his eyes upon er rather than the stage.

Each time it happened he gave an enigmatic smile, and vhen during the interval she queried the empty seat beside

them he said, 'That would have been Cheryl's seat. I didn'
ask you along because we'd got a spare ticket. Satisfied?

She nodded, aware that she'd got it wrong again, bu
only in the matter of a theatre ticket...not about anythin
else.

On the way home Daniel fished a small gift-wrappe
parcel from under the car seat and thrust it into her hands

'Merry Christmas,' he said as she gazed at it in surprise
'And you mustn't open it until Christmas morning.'

'Right,' she agreed solemnly. 'And when we get back t
my place I have something for you.' She turned to Jona
'Would you like to come in for a coffee?'

He shook his head. 'I think not, thanks just the sam
I'm expecting a phone call later, and it's way past th
young man's bedtime.'

She supposed he could have added 'and your fath
won't be best pleased to see me' but he didn't. She wa
pretty sure he was thinking it, but he didn't say it.

'Hold on a moment, then,' she said as he pulled into th
drive. Slipping out of the car, she went to get Daniel'
Christmas present...and the small gift she'd bought fc
Jonas.

As the boy accepted the parcel eagerly and began to fe
it all over through the wrapping, Gemma held out the pacl
age with the Christmas CD in it and said awkwardly, 'Th
is for you, Jonas. I hope that Christmas will be all you wa
it to be.'

He was staring at her, surprise in his eyes and somethin
else she wasn't sure about.

'Do you?' he said quietly. 'Do you really?' And then, ;
if putting a solemn moment behind him, he smiled. 'Than
for the thought...and do I have to wait until Christm;
morning, too?'

'Absolutely,' she told him, returning the smile.

As they drove away she stood watching the car disa]

near. They had actually spent an evening together without any misunderstandings or bad vibes, she thought as she went inside at last. Was it due to Daniel's presence or Cheryl's absence?

Once more under the covers in her bedroom, her father's words of earlier that night came back to mind. He'd called Jonas 'a second-hand Joe' but he was wrong. As far as she was concerned, he had always been first, but, then, who was *she*—just the understudy?

As she was about to slide over the edge into sleep her words to Jonas when she'd given him the gift came back to her. She'd told Jonas that she hoped his Christmas would be all he wanted it to be, but he hadn't returned the wish.

Maybe he thought it was a foregone conclusion in her case, with her father and Roger for company on the Isle of Man. She gave a sleepy groan. If that *was* what he thought, how wrong could he be?

CHAPTER TEN

IN THE week of Christmas it became clear, as it always did,
that nature, with its cruel tricks, and the fates, just as mean
and unpredictable, were not admitting that the festive season was fast approaching.

Accident and Emergency was as busy as ever. The theatre lists were as long as usual, and the clinics had no fewer
outpatients than was normal.

'Why can't they all get better and go home?' Peter said
tetchily one morning as he endured the after-effects of the
party he'd been to the night before.

'The patients haven't asked to be in here at this time of
year,' James reminded him mildly, 'and the nursing staff
are trying to get as many as possible discharged by
Christmas Eve.'

Gemma had told him that she would fill in for him on
Christmas Day and it had been worth it to see his delight.

'But it's on one condition,' she'd warned him.

'Anything.' He'd beamed. 'Just name it.'

'That you don't tell anyone that I'm doing your hours
until the last minute. My father thinks I'm...er...staying
with friends over Christmas and I want it to stay that way.
He's made plans of his own but he'll cancel them if he
discovers that my arrangements aren't quite what I've led
him to believe.'

James had frowned worriedly. 'Are you sure you want
to do this, Gemma?' he'd questioned. 'It all sounds a bit
bleak as far as you're concerned.'

'Yes, I'm quite sure,' she'd told him evenly. 'Go and

hone your wife to tell her that you'll be with her and the
ildren on Christmas Day after all.'

It was in the middle of that same afternoon that Gemma
as surprised to see Sep and Daniel walking towards her
ong the hospital's main corridor.

'To what do we owe this honour?' she asked with a
elcoming smile as they drew near.

Daniel appeared to be his usual self but Septimus looked
hite and drawn.

'I've had a message to say that my mother was brought
an hour ago. There's been a fire at her house.'

'She'll be in Emergency,' Gemma said quickly. 'Would
u like me to come with you?'

'Yes. If you wouldn't mind,' he said raggedly. 'Or al-
rnatively I could leave Dan with you while I find out
hat's happening.'

'We'll go there together,' she suggested, 'and then I'll
ke Daniel to the restaurant for a Coke or something while
u stay with your mother. I don't think his father is in the
spital at the moment.'

'No, he isn't,' Daniel confirmed. 'Dad has gone looking
houses.'

Gemma's heart sank. So he *was* moving house and there
uld only be one reason for that.

When they saw the injured woman it was immediately
ear that she would need to be hospitalised. Sep's mother
as in a state of shock and was being given intravenous
uids through a drip in her arm.

The doctor in Emergency told him, 'The effect of the
cond-degree burns your mother has received has led to
wered blood pressure and a very rapid pulse, caused by
ss of body fluids.'

He pointed to the drip in her arm. 'As you can see, we're
eating that problem, but there are others to consider. The

worst affected areas are her face, neck and upper arm
which she must have raised to try to protect her face.'

A nurse was bending over the injured woman and h
went on, addressing himself to them both, 'The affecte
areas are being cleaned with sterile warm saline and whe
that has been done we will apply antibacterial dressing
probably of silver sulphadiazine.

'I'll be having the patient transferred to the ward late
but for the moment we don't want to move her. We'v
inserted a urinary catheter and given her morphine to con
trol the pain. It's very important that we maintain the bloo
volume for the first forty-eight hours by replacing fluid a
the same time as it is being lost from the body.'

Sep's face was haggard as he told them, 'I got a messag
to say that there had been a fire at my mother's flat. Th
neighbour who phoned me mentioned something about th
place having been recently rewired, but I don't know th
full circumstances.'

His voice broke. 'I wish Jonas were here.'

The other doctor was eyeing him in some surprise. 'I
the young man referring to Jonas Parry?' he asked.

Gemma nodded. 'Yes, Sep is employed by Jonas to loo
after his son, amongst other things.'

'I see. Well, the situation is this. Mr Parry isn't require
at the moment. We in Emergency are dealing with all th
aspects of immediate treatment that your mother require
but in a few days' time it will be his turn to evaluate wha
amount of skin grafting will be required.'

He smiled briefly. 'Our plastic surgery unit is the rea
guard who's left to pick up the pieces.'

Sep nodded grimly. 'My mother's Christmas is going t
be a painful affair, isn't it?'

'It looks like it,' the doctor agreed, 'but take heart. Th
burns are bad enough...but I've seen much worse.'

They had left Daniel outside in the waiting room an

now Gemma suggested, 'I'll leave you with your mother for a while, Sep, and take Daniel for something to eat. Can I bring you anything back?'

'No, thanks. I couldn't eat a thing,' he muttered as the nurse moved away from the bed, her task completed.

'We'll be back soon,' Gemma promised, and while a subdued Daniel ate the sandwich she had bought for him she pondered on what to do next.

No one knew where Jonas was and Sep was in no state to look after his son. At the moment she was on her lunch-break so wouldn't yet be required to return to the wards. If she couldn't get Jonas on his mobile, maybe the best thing would be to take Daniel home and let him stay with her father for the time being.

There was no answer when she tried to reach Jonas, and she concluded that he'd probably left the phone in the car while he was viewing whatever property had taken his eye.

'I can't reach your dad,' she told the boy, 'and Sep will want to stay here with his mother, so how would you like to go to my place for the afternoon? My father will be there...and he loves playing games. We've got Monopoly and Scrabble and you can watch TV if you want.'

He nodded. 'Yes, I'd like that. When can we go?'

'As soon as you've eaten your sandwich and drunk up.'

Her father's face brightened when he saw them, but it sobered when she explained why they were there.

'Of course Daniel can keep me company,' he said jovially. 'Has he had his lunch?'

'Yes. He's had a snack.' She glanced at her watch. 'I'll phone as soon as I've contacted his dad.' She patted the boy's head and said, 'Keep an eye on my dad. He likes to win.'

Her father's deep laugh bellowed forth. 'Are you saying that I'm a cheat?'

Gemma laughed back at him. 'No. I'm just pointing out that you sometimes bend the rules.'

As she left the room he was already telling an eager Daniel where they kept the games, and she drove back to the hospital knowing that one immediate problem had been solved.

It was a minor one, though, compared to what had happened to Sep's mother, and before she presented herself on the wards Gemma paid a quick visit to Emergency.

The injured woman was conscious and, with all visible parts of her swathed in dressings, was talking weakly to her son. When Sep heard Gemma's footstep behind him he turned a ravaged face to her and said hoarsely, 'From what Mum says it sounds as if she's been employing some very inefficient electricians to do some rewiring at her flat. She awoke this morning to find the lounge ablaze...and the only way out was to go through it.'

'Does she live alone?'

'Yes. My dad died five years ago. We had a big detached house in Wimbledon but Mum sold it last year and moved into a retirement flat not far from here.'

'Which I suppose is understandable, as you appear to be doing your own thing.'

Sep was turning back to his mother. 'This is Dr Bartlett, Mum,' he said gently. 'Hers is a name that we hear a lot at the Pimlico apartment. Jonas thinks she's fantastic and young Dan loves her to death.'

Gemma went scarlet. A joke was a joke, but exaggerating at a time like this!

'I doubt it,' she said flatly.

'It's true,' he said briefly as he bent his head to hear what his mother was saying.

'I have to get back to the ward,' she informed him, 'but I'll pop down later when I have a minute, and if Jonas appears I'll tell him where you are—and where Daniel is.'

As she whizzed up the stairs to the wards Gemma was thinking that maybe by the time Jonas collected his son her father might have been captivated by at least one member of the Parry family. He would be a hard man to please if he wasn't.

Sally Graham was going home for Christmas and was delighted at the prospect. Her face was beginning to assume more normal proportions and the wiring was to be removed on Christmas Eve.

She was still far from recovered but she was getting there. To her parents and her staunch boyfriend, who seemed to have forgiven her brief dalliance, the difference was miraculous, and her father had remarked a few times that he was sorry for blowing his top when he'd first seen her.

But there were still those who wouldn't be back in the bosom of their families for the festivities, and Gemma vowed that no matter how down in the doldrums she might feel over Christmas she would do her best to cheer up those who had a lot more to be miserable about than she had.

It was almost five o'clock when Jonas appeared, and he had Cheryl with him, which Gemma supposed wasn't surprising if they'd been viewing properties they would be sharing. But it was not the time for glum surmises.

'Sep and Daniel must have gone out somewhere,' he said when he came breezing into the staffroom as Gemma was on the point of leaving. 'We've been back to the apartment but there was no one there, and I couldn't linger as I have just the one appointment at five-thirty.'

'Yes, they *are* out,' she said in a monotone she wouldn't have used if the expensively dressed Cheryl hadn't been hovering at his heels.

Dark brows rose. 'You know where they are?'

'Yes. Sep is downstairs in Emergency. His mother was brought in with second-degree burns just before lunch.'

'Oh, dear!' he exclaimed. 'And where's Dan?'

'As I couldn't get hold of you I took him to my place. He's with Dad.'

'You really are a gem, Gemma,' he said gravely. 'I'm sorry that you couldn't get hold of me. I'll make sure it doesn't happen again.'

What was that supposed to mean? That he would always be available to her? She thought not!

'Where did you say Sep was?' Cheryl asked with uncharacteristic anxiety.

Gemma stared at her. Was this to be a first? Cheryl showing concern for someone other than herself?

'Downstairs in Emergency,' she repeated, and was further amazed to see the girl open the door and make a quick departure.

If her action registered with Jonas he gave no sign. Instead, he said soberly, 'I'll go down there myself in a moment.'

'Sep was wishing you were here when they brought her in,' she informed him, 'but the doctor on the unit explained that we are the follow-up team and that her need for us will come in a few days' time.'

'Quite so,' he agreed, 'but I must go and give the lad moral support. After that I'll see my five-thirty patient…and then I'll relieve your father of the presence of my son.'

'I'm off,' Gemma told him. 'I'll see you when you come for Daniel.'

'You will indeed…and, Gemma, thanks again. You're always there when I need you.'

'Don't mention it. ''They also serve who only stand and wait'',' she said drily, thinking that those two had been having an exciting time house-hunting while she'd been supporting Sep and seeing to it that Daniel was being looked after.

She was moving towards the door but he pulled her back. 'What's that supposed to mean?'

'Work it out for yourself.'

'No. I want to know what it is you're waiting for.'

He bent suddenly and as his mouth hovered over hers he said softly, 'I don't flatter myself that it's this, but it seems too good an opportunity to miss.'

Two pairs of dark eyes assessed each other for a split second and then it was too late to draw back. Jonas's arms came around her and as he bent to possess her lips he swung her off her feet, crushing her to him as if he'd forgotten that another girl, who was firmly slotted into his life, was in the same building.

Gemma hadn't, though, and much as she would have liked to take the wind out of Cheryl's sails by letting her find Jonas and herself in a passionate hold she couldn't do it.

'Cheryl will be back any second,' she told him breathlessly as she steadied herself on legs that were shaking, 'And if *you* have no shame, *I* have.'

'You and I need to have words,' he said grimly as he straightened his tie. 'For someone who has all the makings of an excellent doctor you aren't very good at seeing what's in front of your nose.'

'Oh, no!' she hooted scornfully. 'And I suppose *you* are!'

'Not always. I was too blind at first to see that you had an affection for me from all that time ago, but I suppose I could be excused for that as I didn't realise we'd met before.'

'And since then?'

He shrugged. 'Sometimes I think I see into your mind…and other times nothing is clear. I said that we should talk and I meant it. When are you flying to the Isle of Man?'

'Er…late on the afternoon of Christmas Eve—tomorrow.'

'It must be before then.'

'There won't be time.'

'No? We'll see, and now I must go to see Sep and his mother or my patient will be here before I've spoken with them.'

'This is a great boy you have, Jonas,' Harry said with genuine heartiness when he called to pick Daniel up. 'I can see why my daughter thinks so highly of him.'

But you still don't see why I am equally entranced with his father, Gemma thought wryly as Jonas acknowledged the compliment with a smiling nod.

'I beat Grandad Harry at Monopoly but he was the best at Scrabble,' Daniel told them.

'Grandad Harry!' Jonas echoed. 'And where has that come from?'

Her father's cheeks reddened. 'The lad had to call me something and that's what we agreed on.'

'Fine,' Daniel's surprised parent said easily, as if he and the retired GP were the best of friends. 'And now we must go, young man. Your other grandad and Michaela are coming round tonight, and they'll wonder where we are if they arrive to find the apartment in darkness.

'Thanks again, Gemma,' he said as she went to the door with them. 'For everything.'

Did that include those moments in the staffroom? she wondered as the car moved off into the dark night.

Her father had gone to bed and Gemma was watching a play on television when the phone rang.

'Sorry to ring so late, Gemma,' Jonas's voice said when she picked it up, 'but I've been thinking about tomorrow. I can't expect Sep to be around for Daniel under the circumstances. Do you think ''Grandad Harry'' would mind having company again?'

'I'm sure he'd love it,' she said after a surprised moment of silence, and Jonas guessed that the pause had been because there was someone else he could have asked.

'You're wondering why I haven't asked Cheryl, aren't you?'

'It did cross my mind,' she admitted, 'but I'm sure you have a very good reason. With regard to Dad having Daniel here with him, do by all means bring him round. But bear in mind he'll only be here until late afternoon. The Isle of Man flight leaves at six o'clock. *I'll* be finishing at the hospital as soon as the lunch-hour is over, which will give me ample time to get ready for the airport.'

She didn't explain that it was only getting ready to go to the airport she was referring to. Once she had seen Dad and Roger airborne she would be coming back home.

'Yes, of course. I understand. I'll pick him up about one-ish. I'll be free myself by then,' he said stiffly. Continuing in a similar tone, he said, 'I didn't ask Cheryl to mind Daniel for two reasons. Firstly, because she has a couple of clients booked in for beauty treatments that I don't want her to have to cancel as she's so rarely occupied, and, secondly, as you are aware from past happenings, she's not Danny boy's favourite person.'

Gemma found herself glaring into the receiver. So he was admitting it at last. That he was prepared to allow someone that his son didn't like to take over a major role in their lives.

'I *am* aware of that fact,' she said coldly, 'and I'm relieved to know that you are, too, which makes it all the more amazing that you're still prepared to jeopardise your son's happiness in pursuit of your own lusts.'

There! It was out! She'd said it and was appalled at her own bluntness.

'"In pursuit of my own lusts"?' he repeated furiously 'That'll be the day! But these are matters I'm not prepared to discuss over the phone. Or at any other time in view of your opinions on the matter.' And he replaced the receiver with a dismissive click.

As Christmas carols chimed out on the heels of the play she'd been watching, it was just another turn of the knife that she was getting to be so adept at twisting for herself.

There had been a chilling finality in Jonas's voice that made her wonder if he would bring Daniel round tomorrow Had she blotted her copy book to such an extent that he was going to break communications between them altogether?

He couldn't do that, though, could he? Even if all contact outside the hospital was severed, Jonas couldn't get away from their job commitments. Health care held them securely in its grasp, but her last gloomy thought before falling into a restless sleep was that neither of them had to stay where they were. There were plenty of other hospitals to choose from.

Gemma had informed her father over breakfast that Daniel might be coming to keep him company again and his face had lit up.

'It isn't definite,' she'd explained, 'but there is a possibility. Sep usually looks after him during school holidays, but at the moment he will want to be with his mother.'

'Aye, well, if the lad comes it will be grand…and if he doesn't it's not the end of the world. But I hope you've told that man of yours that I'm off to the Isle of Man later today,' Harry had said.

'Yes. He knows, and he'll be picking Daniel up at lunchtime…if he brings him. Jonas won't want to be taking up your time, so the moment you hear the car outside send Daniel out to him.'

Her father had described Jonas as 'that man of yours'. He had no idea how far it was from the truth. The man in question was furious with her, but the situation did have its dismal advantages.

The less he had to say to either of them, the less likely he was to find out that she wasn't going away for Christmas. Hence her suggestion that Daniel not be allowed to linger when his father came for him.

And now, after being on the wards for the first half-hour of the day and as yet having seen no sign of Jonas, she was giving her father a quick ring to see if Daniel had arrived.

'Yes. His father dropped him off a quarter of an hour ago,' he said with a lift to his voice. 'And he's brought some games with him.'

So Jonas hadn't taken the hump completely, she thought as she hung up, but it would be time to decide just how angry he was when they met face to face.

On this Christmas Eve the atmosphere was as festive as it was ever likely to be in a place where the trauma of illness held sway.

Peter French, in one of his more mellow moments, had brought in a bottle of sherry, and they all had a glass in the privacy of the staffroom.

Christmas lunch was being served in the restaurant for all who wished to partake, and a brass band from one of the local high schools was going from ward to ward, playing carols.

Cheerful though the atmosphere was, when they played 'It Came Upon the Midnight Clear', the carol that everyone knew was her favourite, Gemma felt like weeping.

'Isn't Jonas coming in today?' she'd asked casually of James as they'd sipped the sherry.

'I'm not sure,' he'd said. 'There's a luncheon later on for all the high-ups in the administration suite. I imagine he'll be going to that. Perhaps he's coming in later.'

Peter had been tuning in as usual and had volunteered, 'If you're wondering where our leader is, he's doing a home visit to a private patient—an aging politician he recently gave a face-lift to. Once that's done he's off to start the Christmas break.'

After that the morning seemed to crawl, and when Gemma left the hospital at lunchtime she quickly pointed her car homewards in the hope that she might get a glimpse of father and son before Jonas departed with Daniel.

But even that small pleasure was not to be allowed her. They had been and gone. When she asked if there was any message, her father looked at her in surprise.

'No. I sent the boy out straight away as you said, and Jonas shouted across that he hoped I would have a nice Christmas and then drove off.'

For once he wasn't tuned in to her mood. He didn't see the weary droop of her shoulders and the tired lines around her eyes. Harry's thoughts were on a track that was running in a different direction.

'How many shirts should I take with me?' he was asking. 'And which of my top coats?'

As she'd been on the point of leaving the hospital James had appeared at her side with a huge bunch of flowers, and when Gemma had eyed him in surprise he'd said, 'Just a thank-you for tomorrow. I'm so grateful.'

He'd hesitated and she'd guessed what was coming next. 'I just wish that you being able to do my hours tomorrow didn't mean that *your* Christmas is going to be so uneventful.'

He'd hesitated again and this time she hadn't been prepared for what had come next. 'My wife says when you've finished here will you join us for Christmas dinner? We'll be sitting down about half past six.'

Gemma had fought back tears. It was typical of the man and his family that they should have been concerned about her being alone. But there had been no way she'd intrude into their family gathering, and with a breezy smile she'd been proud of she'd told him, 'Tell your wife thanks for the offer, James, but I've already accepted an invitation from my neighbours.'

It hadn't been true, of course. The young couple next door were going to his parents in Cardiff, but it had had the desired effect on James. His brow had cleared and he'd given a sigh of relief.

When he and Daniel got back to the apartment Jonas sat gazing thoughtfully into space. He'd deliberately avoided Gemma today, but it didn't seem right that they should each start their Christmas with hurt and anger inside them.

His son had said on the way home that 'Grandad Harry' had told him that he and Gemma were setting off for the airport at three o'clock, and on a sudden impulse he got to his feet.

If they arrived at the airport to see them off, Gemma would at least know that he bore her no ill will, and almost before the thought was born he was picking up his car keys and telling Daniel to put his jacket back on. Within seconds they were weaving in and out of the London traffic.

They were actually on the airport concourse before he admitted to himself the futility of what he was about to do. He could see the three of them in the distance among the throng of last-minute travellers and knew that going there had been a mistake.

Harry was easy enough to pick out, his white thatch caught in the airport lights, as was the neat figure of the young GP beside him, but it was the woman who was with them—dressed in a scarlet wool coat that reached her calves and swirled around her like a bright banner—who had his complete attention.

She was smiling, the warmth of her regard taking in the

two men beside her. Telling himself that he would feel the
world's biggest fool if she were to turn and see him, Jonas
said tightly to his son, 'Come along, Dan. Let's go home.'

'Sure, Dad,' the boy said compliantly. He didn't know
why they were there in the first place and he'd been so
busy looking out for departing or arriving aircraft that he
hadn't seen the party waiting for the Isle of Man flight.

Driving back home, Gemma was thankful that she didn't
have to smile any more. Her face ached with the effort of
trying to look cheerful.

Once her father and Roger had boarded the aircraft she
had walked slowly out of the airport to where she'd parked
her car, and it was then that the reality of what she was
planning had hit her.

She had deliberately chosen to spend Christmas alone
and was now being left to get on with it. There was a small
turkey breast in the fridge, an assortment of vegetables,
some bottles of wine, a purchased Christmas cake…and
that was it.

Her father had given her money to spend as she wished
and her only other gift was the present Daniel had given
her with the solemn warning that it hadn't to be opened
until Christmas morning.

She wondered what it would be and wished that his father had thought fit to remember her at Christmas-time.

At ten o'clock she fell asleep in front of the television,
gratefully thinking as her eyelids drooped that it was one
way to shut out the bleak feeling of limbo that was washing
over her.

It was quiet in the apartment in Pimlico. A subdued Sep
had returned for the night in an anything but festive mood,
even though his mother was progressing as well as could
be expected.

When Daniel had gone to bed, convinced that he would never go to sleep and immediately proving otherwise, the two men sat watching TV, each immersed in sombre thought.

The phone rang and the student au pair was on his feet in a flash, but it wasn't the hospital calling. 'It's for you,' he said, passing the receiver over to Jonas. 'Some guy from the Isle of Man.'

'Harry Bartlett here,' the voice at the other end said. 'I'm calling to make sure that my daughter is safely settled in with you for the next couple of days.'

Jonas goggled at the receiver but, managing to conceal his surprise, came up with a reply of sorts. 'Er...yes...Mr Bartlett.'

'Can I speak to her, then?'

'She's in the shower at the moment.'

'Ah, I see. Well, give her my love, will you? And tell her that we've arrived safely.'

'Yes. I'll do that,' Jonas said obediently as he grappled with the implications of what the other man was saying.

'Is that young lad of yours still up?' Harry asked.

'I'm afraid not.'

'Aye, he'll have gone early, I suppose, with it being Christmas Eve. Tell him Grandad Harry sends his love, will you?'

'Why exactly have you told him to call you that?' Jonas asked carefully.

'Why?' the retired GP repeated. 'Because that's what I'll be...as near as dammit...when my daughter and you get around to naming the date. That girl loves you deeply. I'd rather she didn't, but that's the way it is, and I have to admit that the more I see of you the more I can understand why no other man will ever attract her attention.'

'Thank you for saying that,' Jonas told him. 'Thank you

for everything, Mr Bartlett. You've given me the bes
Christmas present I could ever want...or have.'

'What's that you're saying?' Gemma's father asked
'Something about Christmas presents?' But Jonas wa
wishing him a jubilant farewell and reaching for his coa
off the hall stand.

A strange sound brought Gemma out of sleep and for a
moment she couldn't tell what it was, then it registered
The clear notes of a trumpet could be heard outside in the
dark night.

That was amazing enough, but it was what the trumpeter
was playing that made her catch her breath. The clock on
the mantelpiece showed that it was five minutes to twelve
What could be more fitting at that moment than the sound
of 'It Came Upon the Midnight Clear' breaking into the
silence of Christmas Eve?

Her heart was thudding in her breast as she went to the
window and pulled back the curtains. She knew of only
one man who played the trumpet, and until this moment
she'd never heard him perform, but he was making up for
it.

Standing straight and still in the light of a winter moon,
beneath the frost-festooned branches of a tree and with his
mouth pursed around the cold brass of the trumpet, Jonas
played on until the last notes of the carol she loved died
away.

Then she was running—down the hall, through the front
door and into the arms that were waiting for her.

'How did you know I was here?' she breathed as he
cradled her to him.

His lips were on her brow, his hands gently smoothing
the hair back from the face looking up at him.

'Your father rang to see if you were settled in at my

place and, fool that I am, I at last started to put two and two together and realised that you must be here...alone.

'I'd asked you twice to spend Christmas with Dan and me but you'd refused, and I took it that you'd rather be with your father and that GP fellow.'

He traced her lips with a gentle finger. 'Why *did* you refuse, Gemma?'

'Why do you think? I didn't want to be the odd one out in your household over Christmas. What about Cheryl? Where does *she* fit in? Aren't you going to marry her?'

She was firing the questions like bullets from a gun. They'd been locked up inside her for so long she couldn't wait for answers.

'Steady on! One thing at a time,' he said tenderly, 'Of course I'm not going to marry that spoiled little madam. Cheryl has a lot of personality problems and I've been doing my best to straighten her out.'

As Gemma eyed him dubiously he went on, 'All right, I know that she's had a fixation for me...and I've tried not to upset her by pushing her away.'

'Which makes two of us.'

'What?'

'With a fixation for you.'

He frowned. 'Don't compare yourself with Cheryl. When your father told me how you felt about me I was amazed...and flattered. After the fiasco of my marriage I'd never seen myself as a very attractive commodity. It's surprising how that sort of humiliation can change one's outlook.

'But getting back to my involvement with Cheryl. I was furious when she told Dan that she was going to be his mother. Yet I did understand that it was just bravado on her part, or else an attempt to make someone else jealous.

'Most of her problems stem from a childhood where big sister Michaela and she were left to fend for themselves when their parents were killed in an accident and, fond as I am of my father's wife, I don't think Michaela made a very good job of looking after Cheryl.

'Michaela saw to it that Cheryl had all the physical comforts of life but gave her no affection, and she's turned out to be a disturbed young female who thinks that if she isn' asserting herself she won't be noticed. I thought you'd understand that my relationship with her was strictly remedial but you didn't, did you?'

'Of course I didn't. All I could see was that you were letting someone into your life who wasn't right for either Daniel or you, and I was devastated.'

Her mouth was curving into laughter. 'Especially as I'd long wanted you for myself.'

'You've got me! Had me from the moment the toy dinosaur fell out of your pocket in the hospital corridor, but you do know that I come as a package, don't you? That my son comes with me?'

'Of course I do.' She glowed back at him. 'But if you're going to ask me to marry you, please, tell me first that you love me, before asking me to be Daniel's mother.'

His smile was rueful. 'I made a real hash of that, didn' I? I don't know what possessed me to propose to you like that. I wanted you so much that I think my mind must have gone into a state of sheer idiocy.'

With his eyes worshipping her, he said gently, 'Is this any better? I love and adore you, Gemma Bartlett, and wan you to be my wife. And if at the same time you could see your way to mothering my son and any future offspring we might have, I will be humbly grateful.'

'I think I could do what you ask,' she said with equal gentleness, 'as it is exactly what I want, too. But tell me if this is how you feel about me, why were you thinking of moving away? I'm told that you've been house-hunting.

'Yes, I have, and who do you think I would have been asking to share my new home?'

'Me?'

'Yes, you. At least it was until yesterday when you put me so firmly in my place. After that I wasn't so sure.'

'And now?'

'Now my world has righted itself for the first time in years. The woman I love has promised to marry me and my son will be just as overjoyed as I am.'

'And as for me,' Gemma said joyously, 'Christmas has suddenly come alive...even though I *am* working tomorrow.

'Knowing that you love me is the greatest gift I could ever expect to receive and for as long as I live at this time of year this wonderful moment will be reborn.'

'I did have one or two minor trinkets I was intending to present to you with Christmas in mind,' Jonas said with a teasing smile, 'but after the dressing-down I got the other day I hesitated to offer them. I've been carrying one of them around with me for days.'

'Really?'

He took a small jeweller's box out of his pocket and as he lifted the lid Gemma's eyes widened. The solitaire diamond on its velvet bed winked up at her expectantly. Jonas said, 'Shall we place it where it belongs?'

'Yes, please,' she breathed.

When it was safely on her finger Gemma looked up at him. 'There's just one condition if I'm going to marry you,' she said with mock gravity.

'And what's that?'

'That you don't expect Cheryl to be my bridesmaid!'

'I promise,' he agreed laughingly. 'And before I begin to show you how much I adore you, guess where that young lady is at this moment?'

'Sailing down the Thames on an illuminated barge?'

'No.'

'Wining and dining at London's top nightspot?'

'No.'

'Still doing facials and manicures?'

'Definitely not!'

'I give up.'

'She's sitting in my lounge, keeping young Sep company, which prompts me to ponder if there might be a more lasting affection there than the one she had for me.'

'There has to be, if that's how she's spending Christmas Eve,' Gemma murmured, as his hold tightened and the sweet desire which she'd feared had been hers alone fused them into one being.

MILLS & BOON®

Makes
**any time
special**

Enjoy a romantic novel from
Mills & Boon®

Presents...™   *Enchanted*™   TEMPTATION®

Historical Romance™   ⌁**MEDICAL
ROMANCE**™

MAT1

MILLS & BOON

MEDICAL ROMANCE

MOTHER TO BE by Lucy Clark

Dr Mallory Newman had always loved surgeon Nicholas Sterling but when he married her best friend, she was devastated. Now he's back, widowed and with a two year old daughter. Can his determination to win Mallory's heart survive what she has to tell him first?

DOCTORS AT ODDS by Drusilla Douglas

The last person Dr Sarah Sinclair had wanted to see on her return home was orthopaedic registrar Rory Drummond. After all, her unrequited love for him had caused her to leave in the first place. Had time changed anything or were they destined to be just friends?

A SECOND CHANCE AT LOVE by Laura MacDonald

Single mother Dr Olivia Chandler has no choice but to offer locum Dr Duncan Bradley her spare room. His resemblance to her daughter's father is unsettling but as she gets to know him, she finds herself loving him for himself. But is the feeling mutual?

Available from 7th July 2000

MILLS & BOON®

MEDICAL ROMANCE™

HEART AT RISK by Helen Shelton

Luke Geddes' appointment as Consultant Cardiologist brings him directly in contact with his ex-wife, Dr Annabel Stuart. Shocked at her change in appearance, he is dismayed to discover that what he thought was a mutual parting, was anything but for her...

GREATER THAN RICHES by Jennifer Taylor
Bachelor Doctors

Dr Alexandra Campbell is sure that Dr Stephen Spencer won't be able to cope with helping out the inner city practice. Continually at cross purposes, it's not until Stephen puts his life in danger for Alex that she finally discovers her feelings may be deeper than she thought.

MARRY ME by Meredith Webber
Book Three of a Trilogy

Dr Sarah Gilmour's new posting to Windrush Sidings brought back many memories. Seeing Tony Kemp, the love of her life, after eleven years forced her to realise how much he meant to her. Yet, for now, she needed his help as a senior police officer with an unexpected death...

Available from 7th July 2000

FREE

4 BOOKS

AND A SURPRISE GIFT!

We would like to take this opportunity to thank you for reading this Mills & Boon® book by offering you the chance to take FOUR more specially selected titles from the Medical Romance™ series absolutely FREE! We're also making this offer to introduce you to the benefits of the Reader Service™—

- ★ FREE home delivery
- ★ FREE monthly Newsletter
- ★ FREE gifts and competitions
- ★ Exclusive Reader Service discounts
- ★ Books available before they're in the shops

Accepting these FREE books and gift places you under no obligation to buy; you may cancel at any time, even after receiving your free shipment. Simply complete your details below and return the entire page to the address below. *You don't even need a stamp!*

YES! Please send me 4 free Medical Romance books and a surprise gift. I understand that unless you hear from me, I will receive 6 superb new titles every month for just £2.40 each, postage and packing free. I am under no obligation to purchase any books and may cancel my subscription at any time. The free books and gift will be mine to keep in any case.

M0EC

Ms/Mrs/Miss/Mr ....Initials ....
BLOCK CAPITALS PLEASE

Surname ....

Address ....

....

....Postcode ....

Send this whole page to:
UK: FREEPOST CN81, Croydon, CR9 3WZ
EIRE: PO Box 4546, Kilcock, County Kildare (stamp required)

Offer valid in UK and Eire only and not available to current Reader Service subscribers to this series. We reserve the right to refuse an application and applicants must be aged 18 years or over. Only one application per household. Terms and prices subject to change without notice. Offer expires 31st December 2000. As a result of this application, you may receive further offers from Harlequin Mills & Boon Limited and other carefully selected companies. If you would prefer not to share in this opportunity please write to The Data Manager at the address above.

Mills & Boon® is a registered trademark owned by Harlequin Mills & Boon Limited.
Medical Romance™ is being used as a trademark.